HAYLEY REESE CHOW

I0625156

A CHURN IN THE DARK

Whimsical
Publishing & Illustration

Edited by Micheline Ryckman and Deborah O'Carroll
Cover art and Design by Micheline Ryckman
Map by Hunter Ryckman

For Mich, who asked for more.

FISTS CHECKPOINT

LUMEK FINISH LINE

CRION'S INAUGUARAL
RACE ROYALE COURSE

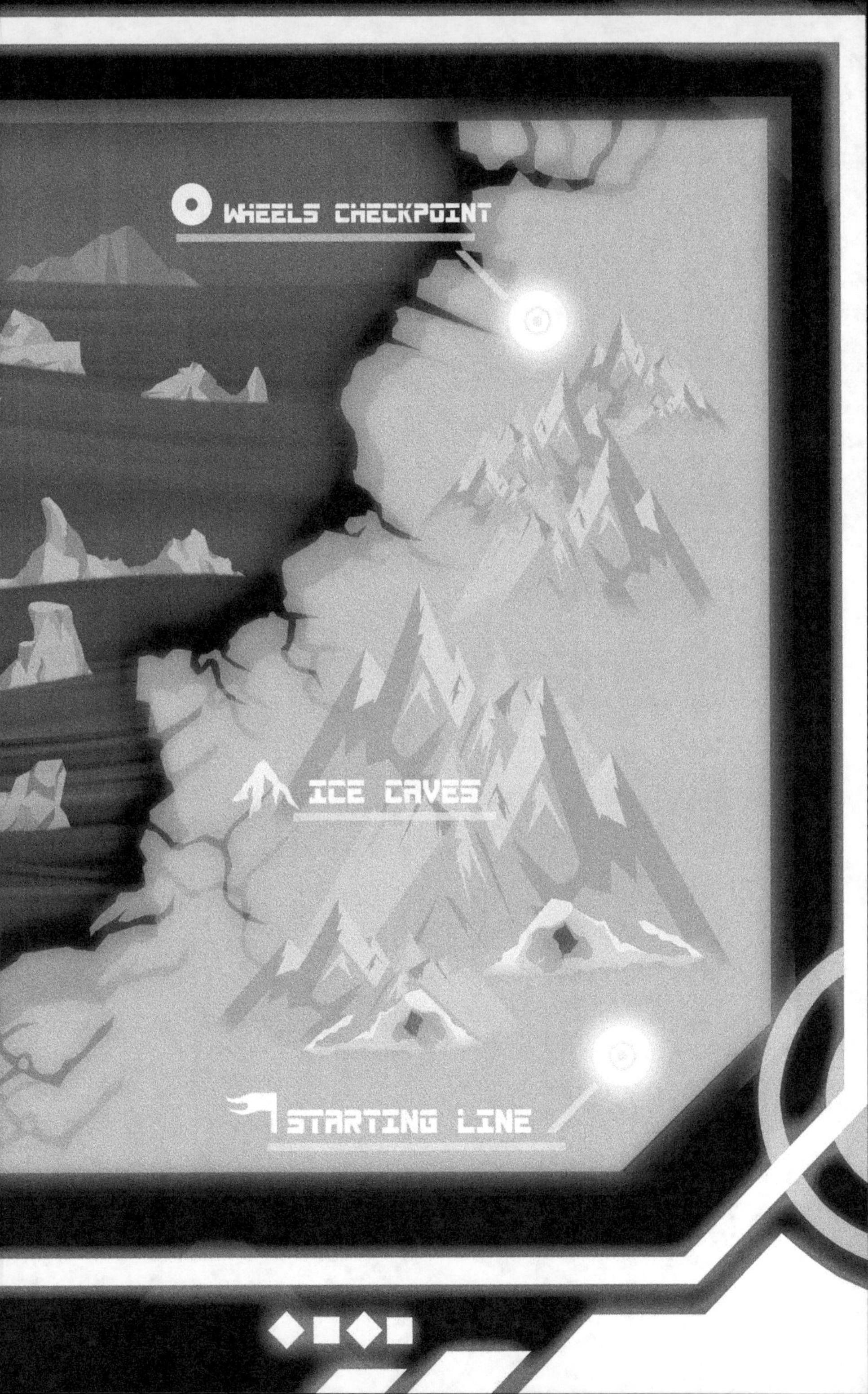

WHEELS CHECKPOINT
ICE CAVES
STARTING LINE

CHAPTER 1

12.29.43B: T-plus 4 months since Mt. Aguya's eruption on Otho

T-MINUS 13 HOURS TO THE START OF THE
INAUGURAL CRIONIAN RACE ROYALE

SYLVIA

THERE WAS no question that Sylvia loved her royalers, but that didn't mean there weren't times when she wanted to strangle them. She stepped onto the lunar hopper's boarding ramp and took a deep breath of the frigid air, letting the stress seep out of her. Hulking mountains of ivory and glacial blue towered around the airstrip in Crion's singular city of Lumik. Above their peaks, a translucent emerald sheen danced across the twilight sky, a continuous aurora courtesy of the terraforming efforts that had finally warmed the atmosphere enough for continuous habitation.

Breathtaking.

On the ground, however, Lumik was somewhat less impressive. A cluster of steep-roofed buildings huddled together between an ice-covered river and the base of the mountain range. Peeking through the drifts of snow hugging their sides, bright holopros of green and red flashed across their smooth facades. The largest one edged the airstrip, its bright decor depicting a variety of pine garlands, wreaths, and boughs in the style of ancient Earthen winter traditions.

Sylvia smoothed the ruffles of her teal-and-purple dress as somewhere behind her, the Amaral siblings squabbled over their strategy for Crion's debut race royale—an argument that had lasted the entirety of the three-day trip. Though the Amarals were currently her fastest rookie royalers, they were also, without a doubt, the loudest. A trait she wished she'd accounted for when deciding which four royalers to bring. With a sigh, Sylvia directed the two hover-dollies carrying their luggage off to their assigned room. *Singular.*

Suns, she wasn't going to survive.

Bex strode past Sylvia in the direction of the host venue, her Belethean formal wear obscured beneath an ankle-length winter coat. "If you think I'm rooming with an Amaral, much less two, you're out of your mind."

"I do feel out of my mind right now, thanks for asking." Sylvia pulled up her schedule, the events flashing out of her goggs in a neat line through the air. She tried to ignore the triple digit number glowing red in the corner—an unwelcome reminder of the unread messages she still needed to address today. "We only have twenty minutes until the opening remarks, so we need to get moving."

They were cutting it close, but the punctuality had been by design. After the Belethea royalers' dramatic success in exposing the events on Otho and saving the system's first complex lifeform, their popularity—already peaking after Sterling/Hart's BRR win last year—had exploded. But even though the Casolla International Federation had initiated a syndicate crackdown to root out the illegal trade of the luxies, the threat of syndicate retaliation loomed large.

As a silver lining, the Belethean royalers no longer needed to fill their schedules with endless promotion opportunities to boost their VSoc cred. Which was good, since it was much safer to spend as little time in the public eye as possible. And while Sylvia abhorred even the possibility of being late, nothing was more important than the safety of her royalers.

Which was why she was resolved not to murder them herself—no matter how irritating they were.

Speaking of the irritants themselves, she turned to find the towering Amarals walking down the boarding plank.

Kit gestured violently with her hands an inch from her older brother's face, her thick lavender braid flying. "Dean, I swear to Casolla, there are going to be land-sea vehicles."

"No way." Dean held up his palm as if to block Kit's face from sight, his lavender mohawk swaying in the gentle breeze. "They're going to be all sea vehicles and make us run up the mountain. Which is why I'm the better choice for the—"

"And that's *enough* of that." Sylvia stabbed two fingers in their direction. "While you were the second highest double ranked going into this race, don't think I won't take a different team next time if you continue to drive the rest of us chaffing *insane.*"

Dean turned his wide lavender eyes on her. "But c'mon, Coach, you have to agree I'm the better sea wheels."

"But he's the worst at adapting to new terrain." Only two inches shy of her brother's 6$'$ 3$''$, Kit shouldered in front of Dean. "Tell him if we're going over ground he has to swap the wheel."

Sylvia pinched the bridge of her nose, trying to remind herself they were lucky to have such top talent on the Belethean team.

Two years ago, recruiting the Amaral siblings would've been unthinkable—even if they were a complete pain in her ass. "Look, you two have raced together since you could walk, and I have complete faith in your ability to make the best decisions for you as a double." They opened their mouths again, and Sylvia cut the air with a hand, her tone dipping into scary-sweet. "But right now, the only thing I'm worried about is getting to the opening remarks, so remember to smile and try not to kill each other on the way."

Unfazed by Sylvia's dangerous proximity to aggravated combustion, the Amarals continued to argue as they followed Bex toward the luminescent gold doors of their venue. Simon stepped beside Sylvia, the small pink ship-cat, Turnip, tucked in his jacket, and a hovercam circling him as he grinned. "I told you to take Chen/Soto."

"You know they're not as fast." Sylvia reached out and scratched Turnip behind the ears, her six tails poking out of Simon's quilted teal jacket. She hadn't fully forgiven the cat for spilling her tea six different times on the flight—a skill Turnip had honed after the last few months with an almost sadistic accuracy—but she was still cute.

"It really is a wonder the Amarals manage to cross the finish line together when they can barely coexist on a day-to-day basis."

"It's their competitiveness that makes them push each other past their limits. They'd both rather sacrifice a lung than lose, and in the race, that's all the common ground they need."

Simon inclined his chin, his dark curls swept back from his forehead. "And the VSoc crowd loves to soak in the drama."

"Well it doesn't hurt that Kit's boyfriend is a crackshot h011ologger who knows how to spin it." Though he and Micah hadn't managed to completely neutralize the Royaler Review's constant spew of garbage, Jabari at least had leveled the playing field. And for that, he had Sylvia's eternal love. If he and Kit ever broke up, she'd probably be crying along with the entirety of the Amaral fanbase. Sylvia raised an eyebrow at Turnip, who looked about ready to fall asleep in the heated lining of Simon's coat. "Speaking of VSoc, are you using my cat for cute points?"

"Of course, Turnip's the only VSoc star on the team bigger than me." Simon tucked her closer under his chin like some ridiculous pink scarf as he continued down the boarding ramp.

"Make sure she stays warm!" Sylvia shouted after him, pushing her curls behind her shoulders.

Simon waved her off as he walked toward the gold doors. "I got it!"

Sylvia shook her head, her lips twitching with affection. What a crew to start the new year with. That just left...

Two strong arms circled her waist, warm lips on the side of her neck. "Think they'll notice if we miss opening remarks?"

Grinning, Sylvia placed her hands on Shiro's, keeping an eye on the time ticking away in her goggs. "You are *such* a bad influence."

"You mean we're not here for a romantic getaway?" Shiro moved to her side, one hand curling around her shoulders as he took in the mountains cutting into the aurora-painted sky. "It certainly looks the part."

Together they strode down onto the airstrip, the boarding plank closing behind them as the lunar hopper automatically taxied to its hangar. "If we're going on a romantic getaway, I want it to be somewhere warm." Sylvia leaned in closer to him to shield herself from what, in comparison to Belethea's gale, was a tame breeze. And yet somehow, it still managed to cut straight through her heated jacket.

Shiro's jaw dropped, feigning shock. "Are you saying we can finally go on a vacation?"

Sylvia wrinkled her nose, a cram-packed calendar lurking a blink away in her goggs. "Maybe in the offseason." Which at a hundred and twenty-five days away, somehow felt too soon and so far at the same time.

Shiro groaned, only half-serious as he whined, "But Ezren and Foster got to skip this one."

"That's because they're not racing, and it was important for them to spend New Year with their families. Especially after everything that happened on Otho."

"You know, I was also on Otho." Shiro smirked with a cheeky smugness only he could achieve. "And it's important for me to ring in the New Year with my girlfriend. Do you think you can arrange that?"

"Oh stop." She bumped him with her hip, her eyes tracking a few other well-dressed spacers walking into the glowing doors ahead of them. "You're already on my calendar."

"I made the *calendar?*" Eyes wide, Shiro straightened his shoulders, exaggerating his swagger. "You must really love me."

Sylvia smothered a smile as they paused at the tall doors adorned with a holopro of carved wood and golden etching. "Just don't forget you have a job to do first. This is the first royale on Crion ever, so there will be people here from all over the system. I don't think anyone would target us without Ezren and Foster here, but I..." Words failed her as she thought of the dark threats that had trickled into the team's inbox in the past week.

"It's okay." Shiro pulled her aside by the door. "I've got that part. You just do your boss-babe-coach thing, and we'll celebrate after your royalers take gold and silver. But first..." He leaned down and pressed his lips to hers, brief and hard and hot. For a moment, Sylvia was lost in him, then he pulled back just as abruptly. "Okay, now you're ready." His eyes danced as he proffered his arm. "Can I escort *the* Coach Sylvia Long inside?"

Sylvia rolled her eyes playfully, her stomach still flipping. "I don't know why I put up with you."

"Because I love you madly with every inch of my soul," he replied, the words almost teasing.

Sylvia barely had time to swat him before they went through the door. Inside, they found a giant lobby with high ceilings and rows upon rows of chairs arranged before a stage. There had to be over two hundred people already seated— spacers in their flashy jumpsuits, Obronians in more tropical attire, and Dreitians in their long robes. The Crionians, she noted, seemed to be making their own statement in thick, knee-length coats with the shifting colors of the aurora patterned into each one. They were certainly trying to carve out a unique name for themselves already.

Shiro slipped her heated coat from her shoulders and tossed it along with his own to the concierge bot. Underneath he wore a three-piece suit with an array of silver chains across the front that perfectly fit his lean body, his gun holstered beneath his jacket. Sylvia couldn't help but take a moment to appreciate his chiseled cheekbones and the unruly black hair she managed to tame on the ship. It wasn't exactly his style, but suns if he didn't wear it well.

She, on the other hand was completely at home in her thigh-high boots and low-cut corset, and she certainly didn't miss the flash of heat in his eyes as he drank in her attire. He offered her his elbow again, but no sooner had they entered the aisle than three hologgers accosted her with a barrage of questions.

"Sylvia, coach of the Belethea royalers, where's Sterling/Hart?"

"Is it true they're racing tomorrow?"

"What can you tell us about the changes they have planned as the two newest members of the BRR council?"

Drawing herself up to her full height, which was generously aided by her three-inch heels, Sylvia gave them a bright smile.

"As we've already stated, Ezren and Foster had prior commitments and will not be joining us here on Crion." She raised her voice over a renewed bombardment of chatter. "However, they did prepare a holopro to congratulate Crion on their terraforming achievements and new planetary status. While Ezren and Foster have officially stepped away from royale racing, as is customary for BRR champions, I'm sure they'll share any BRR council announcements through the appropriate channels."

With that, Sylvia swept across the floor, eyeing the small clock in the corner of her goggs that told her she had only three minutes to get to her appointed spot. Shiro followed close beside her with a giant grin on his face. "I don't know how you do that, but I love it."

"It's all about practice." She shot him a triumphant glance before quickly noting that Bex, Simon, Kit, and Dean were sitting in their assigned row. Excellent, everything was... her smile faded as she spotted her holo-labeled seat right next to Ambassador Villegas. She stifled a groan. "Two minutes to start. You'll check the room?"

"Of course." Now it was Shiro's turn to squeeze her arm. "I'm never far." With that, he turned and strode off through the crowd.

Taking a fortifying breath, Sylvia moved to her seat next to Belethea's black-clad ambassador and bowed. "Ambassador Villegas, what a pleasant surprise. I didn't realize you'd be joining us."

"Well, when I heard that Sterling/Hart wasn't going to be here, I wanted to be sure Belethea had strong representation."

She sniffed, a schedule flicking out from her gold goggs. "Imagine my surprise when I saw them on the agenda."

Sylvia quickly scanned the holopro and internally fumed. Someone had purposely misled the attendees into believing Sterling/Hart would be here in person. "It's only a recorded holo," Sylvia said, already thinking out an angry message in her goggs. "I clearly communicated that to the organizers, but it appears they've chosen their own interpretation. Most likely to stimulate increased interest."

"Indeed." Ambassador Villegas opened her mouth to say more when Crion's Ambassador, Earnest Purcell, took the stage.

"Welcome, everyone, to Crion's first race royale as an official settlement of Casolla..." The ambassador ran a hand through his bushy red beard while he spoke of the importance of the tradition of the race royale, of the recent terraforming technology and funding, and how they hoped, in time, to open the entire planet for colonization. Even Ambassador Villegas got a moment to shine as she rose to give her own congratulatory remarks much to the same effect, the hovercams humming around her.

Purcell turned back to the crowd. "On that note, we invited race royale champion and the new face of terraforming, Ezren Hart, to celebrate this occasion with us. Although she wasn't able to attend in person..." An audible groan rippled through the crowd, and Sylvia's expression tightened. *That's what happens when you mislead people.* "Team Sterling/Hart has sent along this message."

Sylvia finally began to relax as Ezren and Foster's carefully practiced, and perfectly executed, speech played for the crowd. She forced herself not to mouth the words as they spoke of one system united, the pursuit of ethical terraforming, and working together to keep order in the system. Hopefully they were having a relaxing New Year with their families. After all the work they'd been doing lately, they deserved it, and she made a note in her goggs that she needed to check in on them before the day was over.

Technically, Shiro, as the CIF agent responsible for their safety, should've been with them, but he'd rattled off some colorful excuses about risk calculations, and she couldn't be sad that he'd come to Crion instead. With the murderous Ambassador York and his syndicate allies still at large, leaving Belethea always made her nervous. Her gaze flicked to Shiro where he leaned subtly against the wall, his stare calmly roving the crowd. It only took a second for his eyes to meet hers, and he gave her a wink before continuing his scan.

Sylvia's expression smoothed into a smile. It would be fine —if she'd learned anything in the last four months, it was that Shiro was good at his job, and she could trust that her team would be safe with him watching. The clench of her shoulder blades eased, and she used the remainder of the remarks to let herself drift through her overflowing inbox.

She returned to the moment when Ambassador Purcell kicked off the pre-race banquet in the adjacent ballroom. The ambassador knocked his fists together three times with a call of, "Into the churn," and the audience dutifully echoed the words as they rose from their seats, dismissed.

Shiro started toward her, and Sylvia was about to make her excuses to Villegas, when the ambassador nodded toward where the Beletheans were laughing with Greta Sterling's Naris team. Though Greta wasn't there in person, her assistant coach had brought a strong team of four as well.

"I must say I'm impressed with the talent you've been able to recruit this year." The wrinkles around Villegas's hard eyes twitched in what almost looked like approval. "You've done us a surprisingly good turn as the stand-in coach." Sylvia glowed with the unexpected compliment, but before she could reply, Villegas continued, "That said, have you made any headway on recruiting your replacement to cement Belethea as a new force in the race royale sphere? I'm sure your rookies must expect a coach with greater experience than you can deliver, and you'll find no better time to transition than this crest after last year's championship."

Sylvia's mouth flopped open, her cheeks burning now with indignation. "I haven't received any complaints yet, considering my coaching record."

"Yes," Villegas continued, her thin lips pursing in thought, "but haven't your royalers said that Foster Sterling has a heavy hand in the coaching? Your personal royale performance indicates it would be difficult for you to carry his torch once his contract is up at the end of the year. Not to mention, I know you've also taken over team stewardship in the wake of Calderon's step back. That's a lot for any one person to handle."

Sylvia's throat tightened. They were facts, and ones she didn't have planned responses to. With ten new recruits, she *was* drowning in her triple duty as VSoc manager, coach, and team steward, and she hadn't thought ahead yet to when Foster was no longer in residence at Carmella. She swallowed, her gaze flicking to where Shiro now watched the conversation from only a few paces away. "I..." She paused, trying to shove aside her embarrassment. "Those are some valid points, Ambassador, and I'll be sure to explore the options and get back to you on a path forward."

Villegas's weathered countenance softened. "To be clear, Coach Long, I'm not saying you're bad at your job, I'm merely saying if you expect your athletes to grow effectively, you need to have a good team under you—and I mean a management staff, not just your royalers." Villegas held her gaze for a moment, and then nodded, her resting steely expression slot-ting firmly into place. "But you haven't let us down yet, so I'll be eager to see you rise to the challenge."

Sylvia and Shiro both bobbed their heads as Villegas strode off in the direction of the ballroom. Sylvia could only watch her go as she strove to get a handle on her emotions. How had the ambassador's words felt like a compliment and a rebuke at the same time? Over the past year, she'd devoted nearly every ounce of her time and energy into her team. What more did she have to give?

Shiro took a step closer, his voice soft in her ear. "She's not wrong, you know."

Sylvia's glare snapped to him, the confused hurt too fresh. "I don't get where this is coming from. Our royalers are ranked top five in the system, and I've been juggling everything just fine." Okay, with massive amounts of anxiety, and a dropped ball here and there—but she'd been making it work all the same.

"I know you have." Shiro reached out and tugged on one of the curls tickling her shoulder. "VSoc extraordinaire, team steward raking in sponsors and balancing finances, coach guiding workouts and strategy and academics." He smiled, but it held a bittersweet edge. "I've been watching you do it all for months now. Working sixteen-hour days, one-hundred-hour weeks." He cupped her cheek, his thumb stroking just under her lashes—the sleepless shadows that no holopro or makeup would be able to cover completely. "But at what cost?"

"I..." Sylvia pressed her lips together—each word vibrating in her bones. It was another question she wasn't prepared for. Two in one day? She really was off her game. Could she keep up the pace for the rest of her life? Chaff, did she even want to? She'd taken on the VSoc manager job as a stopgap while she figured out what she wanted to do after her royale career. But that had been six years ago now. *Six years.* Where had the time gone?

"I don't know," she finally managed. The team was her whole world—draining as it was... what would fill her life if not for them? "I just, I'll figure it out. I always—"

Raised voices cut her off, drawing her attention to her knot of royalers. The Amarals were arguing again, and—

Her eyes widened, taking in the girl in the bulky coat rushing toward them with something in her hands. She flashed back to the explosion at the exhibition four months ago, and her blood ran cold. "Shiro!"

But he was already running.

CHAPTER 2

T-minus 12 hours to race start

Shiro

SHIRO HAD ALREADY SEEN the girl come late with her team, but he had to admit, as another royaler, he hadn't even considered her as a potential threat. He sprinted the distance between them, his goggs executing a lightning-quick scan—no weapons. But then, what was that metal thing in her hands?

He caught her arms just as she raised the steel container, stopping her where she stood not three strides from Simon Grady. "You don't want to do that."

The Pyrrhian royaler looked up at him, and he frowned, something about her sleek dark hair and oval face strangely familiar. Her huge blue eyes swirled with shock, and then fury quick on its heels. "Let go of me!"

The Amarals finally fell silent as they turned to regard the girl with a mixture of surprise and idle curiosity. Bex's expression remained unreadable while Simon's face had gone slack with something akin to horror.

Another visual scan of the girl's attire confirmed that her jacket was simply a thick winter coat. "Sure thing." With a

14

quick jerk of his hands, Shiro wrenched the container from her grasp, and found—a bucket of red paint. *Ah.* Relief coursed through him. He couldn't argue with the classics.

"Give it back," she snarled, grabbing for it.

He stepped out of her reach. "I think it's better if I keep it. You wouldn't want to stain this shiny new floor."

"What are you trying to—" Sylvia stepped forward, and then stopped abruptly, her expression morphing from fear, to shock, to sadness in a blink. "Oh."

"Where's Sterling/Hart?" the girl snapped, her body rigid as if she might attack at any moment. Which, at this point, was fine. As long as their opponent was unarmed, Shiro was more than confident that any one of the Belethea royalers could defend themselves. Chaff, they could probably even defend *him.*

"I saw them on the agenda." The girl's gaze snapped between the royalers as if they were hiding two more human beings between them. "I know they're here."

"They're not." Kit crossed her arms, regarding the girl with a judgmental eye. "Is this another one of those never-terra protesters?"

"No," Simon whispered, scrubbing a hand over his face. "Chaff, she looks just like her."

Shiro looked from Simon to Sylvia, their shoulders curved with matching resignation. "So I'm guessing you know this girl?" He shoved the paint into the hands of a gawking event worker and shooed him toward the exit.

Bex put a hand on Simon's shoulder, her voice strangely soft. "It's Vieve's little sister."

"*Oh.*" Dean leaned over to whisper loudly to Kit. "Genevieve Navarro, she died in the qualifier."

And then it finally clicked for Shiro. The girl was the younger sister of the Belethean royaler who'd been killed by

Calderon in the BRR qualifier two years ago and whose holo had been all over VSoc amidst Calderon's trial. No wonder she looked familiar.

"I know who Navarro is, Dean." Kit punched him in the arm without taking her eyes off the girl. "But why is her sister coming at us with paint?"

"I'm not here for you, Amaral," the girl said. "I'm here for the traitors who work for my sister's murderer."

Shiro moved closer to Sylvia, the pieces slotting together in a less than pretty image.

"It's not like that, Ina." Simon stepped forward, his jaw tight. "Ezren and Foster don't work for him. They're just a part of the Belethea Race Royale Council."

Ina's blue eyes hardened, striking against her olive skin and jet-black hair. "Keep telling yourself that, Simon, but can you explain away how Foster is sitting literally at Calderon's right hand at every council meeting? In *every* press release."

The young Navarro projected holo after holo from her goggs, each one showing Foster on Calderon's right side—at meetings, announcements, public events, fundraisers... Even though Foster had his resting "fod-off" face in each one, Shiro couldn't deny it was an odd coincidence.

"At this point, I wouldn't be surprised if he's been working with Calderon this whole time." She stepped back, her cards laid, and Shiro let himself relax. She was no longer a physical threat, and though a loose circle of onlookers stood riveted to the exchange, none of them looked remotely hostile either.

"That's not true, Martina." Sylvia raised her hands in a placating gesture, but her expression was firm. "We know Lucian Talmadge sabotaged Vieve's topsuit, and Foster was just as devastated about her loss as we all were." Her face softened, and she took a step forward, her gaze flicking to the coach standing only a few paces behind Martina. "I know you're hurt-

ing. Calderon walking free from the trial was unjust, but that's not Ezren and Foster's fault. They did everything they could, and they're still doing everything they can for the race royale and Belethea itself."

"Right. Their stars rise while my sister's cold body rots in the ground." Martina's face tightened, but there were tears in her eyes. "And everyone just accepted it and moved on. Forgetting her."

"Ina, no one's forgotten her." Simon extended a hand toward the girl, the pain in his eyes red and raw.

"You're just as guilty as the rest, Simon Grady." Martina stepped back, the words spilling like poison from her mouth. "She trusted you—trusted all of you—and you let her die." She slapped his hand away, and Bex surged forward. Simon caught her around the middle, holding her back, as the Pyrrhian team and the Amarals lurched toward each other.

Two steps away from a full-out brawl in the lobby, Shiro leapt between them, one hand on Dean's broad chest, and the other on a shorter, beefier spacer.

"Coach Duncan!" Sylvia barked, her voice amplified through her goggs. "Please remove your royaler before she starts an illegal scrap and disqualifies your entire team!"

The stocky coach stepped forward and seized Martina by the shoulders, glaring at his other racers. "I'm sorry, it's been a long day, I think we'll just skip the banquet and get our rest before the royale tomorrow."

"Good. Idea." The words barely escaped Sylvia's gritted teeth.

Martina shook off her coach, her eyes burning through all of them. "Congratulations, Belethea race royalers, reigning champs. I hope it was worth the blood." She flashed a cold smile as the coach practically dragged her away. "Because you're going to drown in it tomorrow."

The coach finally managed to steer the Pyrrhians off through a side hall, and Shiro dropped his arms, his muscles uncoiling. Bex, Simon, and Sylvia exchanged a look of shared trauma, and he had no doubt the chip messages were flying between them. After all, if Vieve had survived, she might even have been with them at that very moment.

Finally, it was Simon who broke the silence with a long sigh. "All right then. How about that banquet?"

"You should really get that girl DQ'd, Coach." Kit's hands fisted at her sides as she glared after the Pyrrhians.

"It's not worth it." Simon bent down to scratch Turnip's head where she rubbed against his leg. "Her sister died, and the murderer is still one of the most powerful people in the system. She has a right to be angry."

"But not at us." Dean straightened his teal suspenders. "Chaff, I bet you anything they'll have it out for us tomorrow."

"I hope they do." Bex turned toward the banquet hall, slipping her hands into the pockets of her suit jacket. "Better to settle it than let the bad blood curdle."

"Every team will be coming at you tomorrow," Sylvia said, herding them toward the social. "You've got the target of a BRR champion team on your backs, and you're currently ranked third—the highest a Belethea team has ever been seated in pre-season."

The royalers swelled under her words, and Shiro had to give it to her—she knew how to motivate them. A message chimed in his goggs.

SYLVIA: Do you think we have to worry about Martina again tonight?

SHIRO: No, it looked like she didn't actually mean to hurt them, and it seems like she got her frustration out, but I'll keep an eye out for her—and anyone else.

Shiro glanced around, but all the gawkers had returned to their business as the Beletheans stepped into the swirl of the crowded ballroom.

Shiro: Are you sure you want to do the social though after all that drama?

Sylvia: I already gave Simon and Bex the option to skip, but they declined. There's always drama, and it's important to show they can't be shaken.

Shiro: Is Simon okay? He looked kind of... rough.

Sylvia: He and Vieve were close, so it's still hard on him.

"All right." Sylvia's schedule flashed out of her goggs. "You all have an hour to eat and socialize. Be sure to smile when you find and thank the sponsors I assigned to you. Race start is at 0700, so you need to be back in our room by 2000 local time. Unfortunately, due to space restrictions, we're all in the same room." A collective groan arose from the group, Shiro included. That was seriously going to put a damper on his plans. "I know—trust me." Sylvia blew out a frustrated breath through her cheeks. "But with Crion's limited accommodations, each team only got one room. Now." She clapped her hands together and made a shooing motion. "Go. Eat. Mingle. Schmooze. And I will see you back in the room in an hour." Her gaze hardened. "And if I don't, I'm leaving you at home next time."

The team dispersed with varying levels of acknowledgment, and Sylvia turned to Shiro, words still spewing out of her mouth at a mile a minute. "The same goes for you."

"You know, we could sleep in the ship instead." He took her hand in his, giving her a grin. "Have it all to ourselves."

She lifted a rainbow eyebrow at him. "Then Kit and Dean would kill each other, and I'd be down two racers for tomorrow."

He sighed. "It was worth a shot."

"Besides"—Sylvia's protective gaze followed Grady/Guns through the crowd—"I feel better being close to them."

And that was the heart of the matter. Sylvia thought as long as she was close by, she could fix everything. But eventually she'd be juggling too many balls to keep anything in the air. "Yeah, I get it. But what if..." Facing her, he placed his hands on her hips, his gaze capturing hers. "I grab us another room tomorrow night... would that be close enough?"

Sylvia snorted. "Shiro, there are no more rooms."

He shot her a grin. "Have a little faith."

"You think you can get a second room when I can't?" She threw her head back with a laugh. "You're on. If you somehow manage to snag one—doubtful, by the way—we can celebrate New Year tomorrow without the Amarals shouting in our ears."

He kissed the back of her hand. "Sounds like perfect bliss to me."

"You're so full of it." She waved him off. "Now I have to get to work and so do you."

She turned away, looking absolutely gorgeous in her boots, and Shiro couldn't resist calling after her. "I love you."

Her wide eyes flew around the room before she turned on him, obviously struggling for a glare but coming out closer to a laugh. "I can't take you anywhere. Now go!"

Still chuckling to himself, Shiro stuffed his hands into his long coat and sauntered over to the buffet as he took in the ballroom. One whole wall was clear, offering an unparalleled view of the mountains and the aurora-streaked twilight above. Honestly, the place was perfect. He ran his thumb along the velvet box in his coat pocket. She would never consider a getaway for just the two of them until the offseason, but he couldn't wait any longer to ask her.

Though many settlers in Casolla saw marriage as old-fashioned, his adoptive grandmother had instilled in him certain values that couldn't be ignored. And one of them was if you met the person you couldn't live without, you swore your life to them. But proposals were no casual thing—it was a life-changing moment that deserved the right scene, and he'd been waiting months for such an ambiance. Ever since he'd caught Sylvia dancing around Carmella's empty kitchen, belting out a song off-key at three in the morning, he'd known he was going to marry her. And if they just so happened to be on a beautiful, remote planet for the New Year... well that was close enough for him.

He scanned the room again, his goggs providing basic background checks on each guest, courtesy of the CIF data-base. As an added bonus, his two neediest royalers, security-wise, were safe and sound at Gerard Y's mansion with the rockstar's own personal security for the entire week. That left him with only four relatively low-risk royalers to look after. It was simply an opportunity he could not pass by. He put together a plate of blue fruits, cheeses, and ice-themed skewers before finding a wall to lean against with a good vantage point.

But would she say yes?

He knew she was in love with him like he was with her, and they'd talked about a hypothetical future together, but... that hypothetical future hadn't made Sylvia's calendar yet. Which left a sliver of doubt he was ready to erase.

He glanced out the window again, marveling at the colors dancing between the blanket of stars. Though he appreciated Belethea's rugged scenery, it had nothing on this place. He just had to make sure Sylvia didn't completely burn herself out before he got a chance to propose tomorrow at the post-race New Year's Eve party.

"How's the course look out there?"

Shiro turned to see Simon and Bex standing beside him

21

with their own plates of Crionian shrimp appetizers. "This is the course?"

"We're actually standing at the finish line. They'll drive us out to the start in the morning, then we race back." Bex pointed to the saddle between peaks as Turnip jumped onto the table next to her. "The brawling arena is up there, and the final leg is down the mountain."

Shiro nodded, still trying to wrap his head around the idea that they did this for fun. "And how long do you think it'll take you?"

"It's a short race tomorrow," Simon said through a bite of yellow-striped shrimp. "So we'll be done in time to doll up for the New Year's Eve party."

"No one's raced the course before, but Ezren's estimates say nine hours." Bex's hand flashed out just as Turnip overturned a discarded plate from the table, catching it before it could fall to the floor. Bex narrowed her eyes at the cat, and Turnip scampered away with an innocent chirp.

"Short, right." Shiro chuckled, his gaze drifting to Sylvia where she talked to a few other ambassadors, the important people of the system orbiting her as if she were the sun itself. "Well, the sooner you're done, the better. Because I have plans with your coach for that party."

"Is that right?" Simon's eyes lit up with the promise of gossip, and he took a giant step closer to Shiro. "And just what are your plans with our coach there, Agent Tanaka?"

"It's none of your business, Grady," Bex said, handing her empty dishes off to a passing server.

Simon feigned hurt. "Oh, c'mon, Bex. We've known Sylvia for years—she's practically a sister to us."

Keeping one eye on Sylvia where she was introducing the Amarals to another coach, Shiro slipped out the ring box. "Well, if she's your sister, I guess I'm going to ask to be your brother." He popped open the old-fashioned box to show the ring inside—an heirloom passed down to his adoptive grandmother and then on to him. He'd never know what it was worth, but to him it was priceless, and he could only hope it would be good enough for Sylvia.

Simon's jaw dropped. "Fod, kin. I didn't know you were serious."

Bex barely seemed to glance at the ring as she turned her gaze back to the mountains without comment.

"What do you mean you didn't know I was serious?" Shiro pocketed the ring once more. "We've spent almost every waking minute together for the last four months."

Simon laughed, expertly flicking a rogue curl away from his forehead. "Well yeah, you're all flirty, but I didn't know it was *this* level. I mean, I don't think I've seen you serious about anything since we left Otho."

Shiro stuffed a shrimp skewer in his mouth, savoring the fresh taste. "I'm only serious when I have to be." Honestly, he'd seen too many gut-wrenching sights not to smile when he could.

"Oh yeah?" Bex glanced at him, her face impassive. "Have you ever told her how you feel about her with a straight face?"

"Um..." Shiro scratched at his hair, trying not to mess up the style Sylvia had spent the better part of an hour working to achieve. "Is the expression important if I meant it?"

Bex rolled her eyes. "Are you going to be laughing when you propose?"

"No, but I might be smiling." Shiro's grin widened as he made eye contact with Sylvia. "It's supposed to be a happy thing, Gunderson."

"If you want to take this kind of oath, then she needs to know you're serious," Bex said, her blue eyes cutting. "After all, Sylvia doesn't make any decisions lightly."

"Aw, don't mind Bex, I'm sure it'll go fine. I mean, it's not like he's asking her to change her life. They practically act like they're married already." Simon clapped him on the shoulder. "If it were me—"

"Don't give him any advice." Bex's stare whipped to Simon. "You're not qualified."

Simon laughed again, holding his hands up in surrender. "Okay. Not wrong. But you're not qualified either." Simon gave Shiro an apologetic shrug. "Commitment and romance aren't really our fortes."

Shiro chuckled again, thinking of Simon blowing up the holologs with new dating rumors every other weekend. And in all the time he'd spent with the team, he'd never even heard a whisper of a romantic tie to Bex. Which meant—he really was on his own here.

"Okay, yeah, but you know Sylvia." He studied one royaler and then the other as he polished off the last of the sugary cheese. "You think she'll say yes?"

Simon shared a glance with Bex, both of their expressions unreadable as something unspoken passed between them.

And Shiro's sliver of anxiety grew three sizes. "Wait. You think she'll say *no*?"

Simon snorted as he leaned on Bex's shoulder. "No offense, kin. We think Sylvia's fritzed for you, but she's kind of already married to the job." Someone called to them from a gaggle of royalers, and he gave another shrug. "Good luck though. We're rooting for you."

Shiro ran a hand through his hair. That hadn't been reassuring at all. Eager to distract himself, he placed his plate on a dining cart and went back to surveillance. Still, as he browsed the information accompanying each face, his mind couldn't help but wander back to the proposal.

Bex and Simon may have known Sylvia longer, but surely

he knew her better. Even though she was doing three jobs right now, once she got a solid staff under her, she would have some more space to have her own life. With him. Just because it hadn't happened yet, didn't mean it wouldn't, and if anyone could think ahead, it was Sylvia.

The word "unidentified" popped up in his goggs, and Shiro frowned. He moved to get a better look at the man in the crisp spacer one piece, but nothing about him screamed out of place. He looked too old to be a royaler, but there was no shortage of politicians, coaches, and press in the room, and if he hadn't popped up as un-ID'd, Shiro wouldn't have noticed him. Casually, Shiro started making his way toward the man, taking holos of him from different angles with his goggs to send to the CIF cyber section for a more rigorous scan. He'd just opened his mouth to call to the man when a sharp voice interrupted him.

"Hey, are you Belethea's coach?"

Shiro turned to see Martina Navarro standing in front of him with her arms crossed. *Chaff*. Wasn't the coach supposed to keep her away? "I'm merely her dashing assistant. You're looking for Coach Sylvia Long, over there." He gestured to where Sylvia stood in her ever-present circle of hologloggers, but she was already looking in Shiro's direction, alarm sparking in her eyes.

"But she's just the interim coach." Martina wrinkled her nose. "Hasn't she hired a real replacement yet?"

His smile tightened. "I suppose there isn't really a rush when Coach Long led Belethea to a BRR title for the first time in... oh, I don't know. Ever?" He tried to keep one eye on the un-ID'd man, but he was making his way toward the exit. "Look, just make life easier on the rest of us and go back to your room before you do something we all regret."

With that, he strode through the crowd, following the man through the door into the bitter cold. He took a step out into the frigid night air, head whipping around, but his frown only deepened. The man must've doubled back. *Shaft.*

For a moment, he only stood there, letting the air bite into his lungs. Martina Navarro was one thing—she was justifiably disgruntled, her motives clear, her identity known... and mouthy as chaff. She could be an annoyance, but the loud ones were rarely the real problem.

He looked back through the glass at the party, but his goggs found no trace of the mystery man. *Concerning.* Shiro crafted a quick message with the holopros of the man's face and sent it to both the CIF and Crion security asking for further information. Even so, he knew at the heart of it, he was really on his own. Crion's security was skeletal at best, and the CIF was too far away to be effective.

In any case, if the man wasn't in the database, he was almost certainly a member of a syndicate. Though he'd be shocked if it was the Kalashnik they'd dealt with on Otho. They'd been mostly dismantled by the CIF in the last few months, and the remnants had gone into hiding. Although Ambassador York, the corrupt spacer ambassador with Kalashnik ties, was still missing, the Kalashnik themselves were now considered a neutralized threat. But they weren't the only syndicate in Casolla, nor were they the most dangerous either... Something about it all didn't sit right.

Especially here. So many high-profile figures in attendance meant no lack of potential targets. And selfishly, the thought brought some measure of relief. The ghost was certainly an ugly shadow waiting to rear its head, but with a little luck, he wouldn't be Shiro's *personal* problem. Shoulders relaxing, he met Sylvia's gaze through the glass, and she beckoned him inside.

There was always the possibility that Shiro was off base. The guy could just be a holologger without an invitation, trying to hide his identity. Or maybe even another security member undercover. Shiro certainly *hoped* the sour feeling in his gut was unfounded. After all, he didn't want anything as small as a chipped nail to ruin his plans for tomorrow, and certainly not a syndicate hitman.

He gave the mountains one last look over his shoulder. The planet really was beautiful—towering blue-and-white peaks reaching up to strafe the perpetually rippling sky. Behind the aurora-bathed slopes, the stars glittered so brightly Shiro had to resist the urge to reach for them—like a million diamonds for a million rings. Nothing like the mere glimpses of the night sky they snatched on cloudy Belethea.

On the whole, it seemed much too quiet to be the stage a hundred royalers would be sprinting and fighting through come tomorrow. Then again, after spending the last few months on Belethea, he knew better than anyone not to trust the calm before the storm.

CHAPTER 3

12.30.43B (Casollan New Year's Eve)

T-minus fifteen minutes to race start

SYLVIA

SYLVIA WAS one stressor away from barfing up butterflies, as usual. Pre-race nerves were a hurdle she had yet to conquer—a snag she'd been battling since she started jetbike racing at four. Strangely, the nerves had gotten easier when she'd upgraded to royaling at twelve. But now that she was a coach, they were worse than ever.

The wind snaked into her hair beneath the hood of her heated parka, the thick layers making her miss her topsuit as she stood behind the crowded starting line. She suppressed a shiver, glad that it was a short race since the topsuit temperature compensation would be sapping a lot of energy from her royalers. While they were all under twenty-one and could certainly handle the strain, she still didn't want them to be too exhausted to enjoy the New Year.

She glanced at the clear blue sky, jade and amethyst twirling amidst the heavens beneath Casolla's huge volcanic face. Chaff, she wasn't sure she'd ever get used to a clear sky and calm winds. But it would make for a quick easy race—no reason for nerves.

"All right, get in here," she called. Bex and Simon stopped their sparring warm up, and the Amarals paused their newest argument to join their circle. Shiro leaned against the wall of the starting outpost, his swiveling gaze pausing on them as a smile tilted his lips.

"Okay, listen," Sylvia said. "I know this is a short race, but your finish here will affect your placement in the BRR qualifier." She squeezed the arms of Bex and Kit on either side of her. "You've done great so far this season, but if you want to cement Belethea's place as a competitor, we have to be consistent. Until then, as far as the rest of the system is concerned, Belethea's just a pretender needing a comeuppance. So watch out for one another at the start. On this team, we take care of each other." She met each of their gazes in turn—Bex's impassive, Simon's cocky, Dean's thoughtful, and Kit's determined. "No matter what happens though, I'm proud of how hard you worked to get here."

"This won't be the time to pace ourselves." Bex turned out to stare at the mountains in the distance. "Without the storms taxing our topsuits, we can afford to run faster."

Kit and Dean shared perhaps the first magnanimous glance since they'd arrived, and then Kit smiled. "You don't need to worry about that."

"But if you really want to keep an eye on us"—Dean winked—"then you'll be looking forward, not back."

Simon burst out laughing, leaning on Bex's shoulder as if they'd just heard the joke of the century. "Oh, rookie, I love the optimism—it's so cute and absolutely ridiculous at the same time."

"Enough," Bex said, her tone as sharp as her icy gaze.

"Belethea's rep is on the line, not just your own, so we're all hoping you can back up those words." Bex turned to Sylvia with a curt wave of her hand. "We'll see you at the finish line, Coach."

"We'll be the ones in front." Simon grinned, turning toward the starting line. "I want a blue umbrella in my recovery shake this time."

"Umbrellas?" Dean asked.

"Don't get him started," Bex said. "Heads in."

Leaving them to their pre-race routine, Sylvia walked back to the outpost to stand beside Shiro, her gaze drifting across the rest of the sixty doubles teams jostling at the holopro starting line gleaming in the snow. The holologgers gathered on the far side of the press line, and though Sylvia probably should've been giving them a remark, she couldn't summon the motivation with the nerves still bubbling in her chest.

She leaned into Shiro's teal parka. "Everything look okay?"

"Completely quiet." He turned toward her, blocking the light breeze with his body. "How're you feeling about their chances? Think they'll place?"

Sylvia pursed her lips. The Beletheans parted from their huddle, and she could tell even from a distance that the Amarals were arguing again. She gritted her teeth. They had approximately three minutes to get it together.

They'd only competed in one other exhibition match back on Belethea, and though both doubles had made the top ten, they'd had their full team at their back and the advantage of course experience. This would be a whole new test. No one had raced here before, and though Ezren had tried to put together some course optimization algorithms based on the researchers' data, judging by the tranquility of the climate, Sylvia doubted it would give them much of an edge.

And if they didn't place, it would be a serious blow to her

royalers' confidence. While hard to quantify, it was no less important than any other stat as they prepped to go into the BRR. Not to mention, it certainly wouldn't do her coaching status any favors in Villegas's estimation.

Still, as long as no one got hurt, that was the most important thing. Anything else they could recover from.

"I don't know, but either way I figure we'll have a sparking good time at the New Year's Party tonight." She flashed him a smile. "It's only the beginning of the season after all."

"My, my, you're relaxed today." Although the words were light, a tight strain flickered behind Shiro's normally calm visage.

"And you seem a little tense."

"Maybe we're rubbing off on each other," he chuckled.

The announcer gave a one-minute warning, and a hush fell over the crowd. Sylvia brought up the royalers' live feeds and wound an arm through Shiro's. Kit pushed Dean, and Sylvia had to restrain herself from marching out there and dragging her from the finish line by her long braid.

SHIRO: YOU THINK KIT AND DEAN WILL MAKE IT WITHOUT KILLING EACH OTHER?

SYLVIA: IF THEY DON'T, I'M NEVER TAKING A SIBLING TEAM EVER AGAIN.

Beside the Amarals, Grady/Guns stood relaxed and ready, like they had dozens of times before. Knocked out early last year due to Calderon's sabotage, this would be their final season of eligibility to prove themselves.

She could see it in their eyes—the desperation to win, to hold on to this, and a part of her still felt it for them. Because life changed after race royale careers. They wouldn't be the same people anymore. They'd have to find their way all over again. Like Ezren and Foster were doing now.

And what about her? She'd never set out to be on the royale

team forever. She'd simply not known what she was going to do after she aged out. VSoc management had been a natural offramp for her BRR passions, but she had to admit, coaching had always felt beyond her depth. And now—she glanced at Shiro out of the corner of her eye—she could imagine a future when the royale, once her entire life, didn't consume her every waking moment. But she knew all too well imaginings didn't always become reality.

Could there be an "after" for her as well? Or would she continue living in Carmella's dorms forever as her royalers came and moved on without her?

Dean shoved Kit back, and she fell straight into Simon. Sylvia tensed. Suns, maybe she *had* picked the wrong double after all. If they couldn't focus, they wouldn't even make the first cutoff.

The announcer started his countdown. *Three.*

Simon righted himself with a glare at Kit. *Two.*

Sylvia had to keep herself from covering her face with her hands. *One.*

Then the four of them were off, but they only took a few steps before a red blur flew at Simon's middle. Sylvia stifled a shriek as three more red shapes entered the scrap along with Bex and the Amarals.

"It's Martina and the Pyrrhians," Shiro said, tense beside her. "Do they usually attack like that at the beginning?"

"They can, but it doesn't make sense in a small, short race like this." Sylvia tried to parse through their feeds to get a sense of what was happening, but it was all chaos and snow. "If they don't—"

"They're up!"

Sylvia's gaze snapped to where Kit pulled Simon from the fray, and they raced after Bex and Dean. Though they left the

Pyrrhians behind, the distance between them and the rest of the royalers was only stretching.

Sylvia pressed her palms into her forehead, her nerves combusting into panic. "I shouldn't have brought Kit and Dean. There's too much tension between them. If Simon had been ready, they could've missed that scrap, and they wouldn't be so behind. What if they don't make the wheels cut-off?"

The Beletheans' feeds flicked out from Shiro's goggs, his expression smooth, as usual. "But they have plenty of time to catch up, right?"

Sylvia ran through the course in her goggs again. "They have to run to the base of the mountains, then the route goes through a cave system. The run is only fifty miles total though." She bit her lip, trying to calculate the odds. "It's not much time, but the cave is a wildcard." Shiro shepherded her toward the research plane that would take them back to the start. "From there, I think they should be okay. They'll have one hundred and fifty miles through icy waters, but we've been practicing on the sims for that. If they make it to the brawl on the mountain peak, they'll be fine."

"So what you're saying is, they'll be fine." Shiro grinned as they climbed onto the small outpost jet with the other coaches and hologgers, all of them transfixed by the many holopros of the royalers glowing in front of them.

Sylvia's lips tightened as the door closed, and the aircraft took off from the ground, speeding them back toward the finish line. "It's dangerous to underestimate a royale even on the clearest of days. The Churn isn't just about the weather, it's about the people."

Barely aware of her surroundings, Sylvia remained glued to her own holos as Grady/Guns and the Amarals scrapped and ran through the open tundra. But when they entered the caves, her anxiety spiked again. Shiro guided her off the plane and into the main viewing room of the venue, where all of the royalers' holos glowed from the walls in front of hundreds of chattering spectators.

With his hands firmly on her shoulders, he led her to the Belethea corner of the display where a dozen other holologgers gathered round. "See, Grady/Guns is already in twentieth," Shiro said, his voice quiet. "They're making up time and legs isn't even their strong suit."

Sylvia watched as the lights from their helmets and the glow of their topsuits led them through the maze of the caves. Technically there were multiple paths they could use to get through the winding caverns, but they'd mapped out their route well in advance. Still, finding their way through it in the dark, when another royaler could round a corner at any second was another problem altogether. As if to prove her point, a royaler's mayday call went up.

"Scrap cracked a helmet on an Exa team," Shiro explained before she could even ask. "How're Kit and Dean?"

Sylvia's brows scrunched together. "Looks like they decided to split up on a different path, but they're not far behind Grady/Guns." She allowed herself a small smile as they passed another team and sidestepped a scrap.

"I'm surprised they're not fighting," Shiro said, their breathless crosstalk projected through the holopro.

"They're too competitive for that." Sylvia drummed her teal-painted fingernails on her chin. "In the end, what makes them fight is also what makes them good. They don't cut each other any slack because they both desperately want to win."

"Then why are you so nervous?" Shiro folded her in a hug from behind, his ease totally at odds with the tension threatening to strangle her.

"I'm always nervous, Shiro." But even as she said it, she

melted into him. Something about Shiro always made her feel safe.

"Are you going to be nervous for the whole nine hours?" he teased, his breath warm against her ear.

"Yes." His hands moved up to her shoulders, his fingers massaging into the knots along her neck. She hummed in pleasure as she read through the hologgers' live reports. The Royaler Review was being predictably obnoxious, but Micah and Jabari were doing an excellent job combatting their vitriol. No surprise there. Micah, as the BRR's self-proclaimed number one fangirl, had shown off her VSoc prowess at every turn. In fact...

Sylvia's brow furrowed. Micah was the perfect choice for Belethea's team VSoc manager. Even the thought of transferring those duties made Sylvia want to cry with relief. Now that the Belethean team was able to pay a competitive salary... She sank her teeth into her lower lip, willing herself not to think too far ahead before she asked the question. But, suns, it was a big hope.

"You know if you insist on stressing..." Shiro's hands continued their smooth movements. "It's a good thing we're going to have our own room so you can unwind."

"I'll believe that miracle when I see it." A notification dinged in Sylvia's goggs with reactions to Ezren and Foster's absence at the race. She skimmed through the article, and its mention of their New Year stay at Gerard's mansion. Shiro wouldn't be pleased that their whereabouts had been pinpointed, but she was surprised to find Gerard had publicly announced that he was staying on Belethea for the near future. There was even a report that Greta Sterling was also at the mansion for the holiday amid rumors that she and Gerard had rekindled their romance.

But... if that was true, did that mean Greta might be

spending more time on Belethea as well? Now that Calderon's direct management of the team had been, for all intents and purposes, forbidden, would she consider taking a coaching position? Because if Micah was her VSoc manager, and Greta was her head coach... then that would just leave her as the team owner's steward—a position that would be in place until Calderon sold the team... or died.

Since Calderon had no blood heirs, Sylvia had no idea what would become of the team or the rest of his assets. The thought sent a bolt of shock through her. Calderon was one hundred and three years old—why weren't all the hapologgers talking about this? Without an heir, there was even a potential that the Belethea race royalers could be disbanded. The breath left her lungs as she watched Bex and Simon run into a dead end and double back. Resolve stole through her limbs like a band of steel. If she wanted to have any say—any power to protect her team—she had to have more authority. But in order to climb the ladder... first she had to free her hands.

"What're you thinking about?" Shiro's chest rumbled against her back.

"The future," Sylvia murmured, squinting to read just how fast the Amarals were moving.

"I think that's an excellent thing to be thinking about."

She could practically hear the smile edging his words.

"Oh yeah?" Sylvia turned to face him, reaching up to sweep his dark hair away from his forehead. "And how do you see your future going?"

"Much like our present." He grinned down at her, mischief glinting in his dark eyes. "Well."

"Any word on a reassignment? With the syndicates and threats quiet, I know they can't let you stay for long." It was a fear that often lay sheltered in the corner of her mind, but the only way she knew to combat it was to speak it aloud.

"Well, there are still some syndicate demons hidden in the crevices of the system, but technically, as of three days ago, my commitment's already paid up, so I'm free to accept or decline whatever next assignment they offer me." His answer was so smooth it felt practiced, and Sylvia wondered how she'd missed this.

"Why would you decline? After all those awards they gave you, I thought for sure you'd want to be looking for a promotion somewhere." Sylvia fought to keep her face neutral. There were few positions that held more clout than the CIF, and their agents traveled all over the system to keep the peace.

"I see myself as the keeper of a pink cat." Shiro planted a kiss on her forehead, eyes twinkling. "Everything else is flexible."

It was another nonanswer. Though she didn't know why she'd expected any different. They'd run similar circles about the future in the past few months. But she supposed she should be happy with the time they had. After all, she could barely get a handle on what her next move looked like, so who was she to judge? Besides, in all the craziness of her life, Shiro was her anchor—her rock. His very presence let her unwind, slow down, take some time to herself.

In the simplest terms, he just made life better. And she would take any time he was willing to give her.

"You know, I really hope you can pull off a minor miracle and get that extra room tonight," she whispered.

Shiro's body jolted to attention so violently, she thought she must've said something wrong. His grin turned almost manic. "And if I do, we get a night off, just the two of us?"

Sylvia chuckled as Grady/Guns passed another double. "After we make a brief appearance at the New Year's party."

"And brief means less than ten minutes."

Sylvia's lips twisted. "An hour."

He crossed his arms. "Fifteen."

"Forty-five."

"Twenty and I up the ante with a hot bath."

Sylvia made a show of caving even as she inwardly delighted at the thought. There was nothing better than a hot bath, especially with the cold night clawing at the windows. "Oh, all right. You have a deal."

"Challenge accepted." Grabbing her hand, he lifted it to his lips. "Now if you'll excuse me, I have a minor miracle to perform."

Sylvia watched her unruly ship captain and team bodyguard stride purposely out the door and couldn't suppress a smile. Even now, she marveled at how he inspired her to reassess her own future. How he could simultaneously make her feel like she could achieve every ambitious whim she'd ever entertained, and yet also make her prioritize her own desires—endlessly supporting her no matter where her current musings took her. He'd charmed the team and her family in turn, fitting seamlessly into her crazy life as if he'd always belonged there. And somehow, no matter how she looked at the future now, she couldn't imagine it without him.

Which was dangerous with their next steps still so uncertain.

And yet, somehow, she couldn't help herself from imagining it all the same.

CHAPTER 4

T-plus 2 hours after race start

SYLVIA

TWO HOURS INTO THE RACE, Sylvia slipped away from the gaggle of hololog interviewers and back to the Belethea royalers' holos. Each set had both of the royalers' live feeds, along with their position on a GPS locator map and their distance to the checkpoints—the vehicle pick-up, the brawl arena, and the finish.

Grady/Guns was now solidly in fourth as they found their way through the caves. Simon, in his usual way, was giving a ridiculous stream of consciousness as he and Bex navigated the icy labyrinth—their goggs but pricks of life in the blackness. The man certainly knew how to entertain the masses.

Meanwhile, Bex ran silently alongside him, yanking Simon to one side to prevent him from impaling himself on a spike of rock. Sylvia nodded to herself. Experienced, dependable, popular, and in tune; pride swelled in her chest. Although they were a ways behind, legs was always their weak point, and they'd done a lot of training with Ezren this year to compensate. Sylvia allowed herself a brief moment to imagine Casolla's

39

shock if Belethea pulled off a back-to-back BRR win. If anyone could do it—it was Grady/Guns. Certainly no one else wanted it more.

But that meant as much as she wanted to watch them climb their way to gold, they weren't the ones who needed her attention.

Her gaze caught a particularly brutal scrap between Naris and Gobrion Stations. A crowd had gathered around the holo, and the chamber echoed with their cheers and yells. She watched until Naris made their narrow escape down a steep tunnel in the opposite direction of the checkpoint, and her shoulders unknotted. While she loved the race royale, after Grady/Guns' close call last year and Vieve's death the year before, she dreaded the buzz of another mayday call. Neither of those things had been accidents, though—they'd been sabotage. But since then, they'd at least forced Calderon to step back from the BRR, and now they had Shiro to protect them. Everything would be fine.

Taking a shaky breath, she pivoted to focus on the Amarals' screen—and her eyes nearly bulged out of her head. They had dropped to forty-five out of sixty teams? *What?* She stepped closer. How had they gotten that far behind? Sure, they'd gotten a slow start, but no worse than Grady/Guns, and the legs were their strong suit. Their goggs cams were so dark, she could barely see what was going on. With a thought, she linked her goggs to the feed and projected the holo in front of her.

Completely dark.

Her blood turned cold. Were their lights not working on their suits? She couldn't hear them talking either.

She looked back at their stats. They'd now fallen to forty-seventh. Had one of them gotten hurt? Fallen down the wrong tunnel? Heart racing now, she pulled up the GPS to see just where they'd gotten stuck. Their tracker wasn't moving. She swallowed, forcing herself to consider the options. Either they really weren't moving, or the transponders on their suits had stopped working. She nearly choked on her hammering heart. Suit malfunction was Calderon's murder weapon of choice.

Surely he wouldn't risk doing this again. And to Kit and Dean of all people. They were rookie racers, in no danger of winning. Her chest heaving, she fired off a message to Micah.

SYLVIA: DO YOU HAVE THE TRANSCRIPTS FOR THE AMARALS? THEIR MARKER ISN'T UPDATING, AND I NEED TO KNOW WHY. IT COULD BE THE SUITS, THE CAVE TRANSPONDER, OR THEY COULD BE HURT OR MAYBE SOMETHING ELSE I HAVEN'T THOUGHT OF. DID YOU SEE ANYTHING? DO YOU HAVE THE TRANSCRIPT OF WHAT WAS HAPPENING WHEN THEY WENT DARK?

Her stomach roiling, she fired off another message to Ezren and Foster. She wasn't sure if they'd be actively watching the royale, but they'd definitely be following it.

SYLVIA: HEY, SOMETHING WEIRD IS GOING ON WITH KIT AND DEAN. JUST CHECKING IN TO MAKE SURE THE TWO OF YOU ARE OKAY AND ENJOYING YOUR NEW YEAR.

It's okay, she reasoned with herself. Even if something was going on, Ezren and Foster could take care of themselves. With the constant death threats coming in after their BRR council placement, they didn't go anywhere unarmed anymore, and Shiro made sure Gerard had plenty of security in place for their stay there. It would be fine. And yet somehow her chest only pumped faster with the possibilities—last year's terrorist attacks ricocheting through her brain.

Micah's message was the first to interrupt her spiraling hyperventilation—no surprise there.

MICAH: I WAS JUST ABOUT TO MESSAGE YOU! THEIR MARKER HASN'T BEEN UPDATING FOR THE LAST SIXTEEN MINUTES AND COUNTING! THE TRANSCRIPT SEEMS LIKE

COMPLETELY NORMAL CHATTER UNTIL IT STOPS. (SEE BELOW.)

KIT: *I SEE ANOTHER LIGHT AHEAD ON OUR LEFT, ARE WE HEADED THAT WAY?*

DEAN: *YEAH, TURN YOUR LIGHTS OFF SO WE CAN GET THE JUMP ON THE SCRAP.*

MICAH: SO THAT EXPLAINS GOING DARK, BUT THEN WE NEVER SAW THE SCRAP HAPPEN. FROM THE OTHER STREAMS, I THINK IT WAS THE HYDRONZA TEAM, BUT WE NEVER SAW THE AMARALS POP UP ON THEIR FEEDS EITHER. RIGHT NOW, THE BEST GUESS ON VSOC IS THAT KIT AND DEAN FELL DOWN A CAVE SHAFT IN THE DARK, AND THEIR MAYDAY DIDN'T SOUND. OR IT SOMEHOW BROKE THEIR TRANSPONDER SO IT'S NOT PROJECTING ANYMORE.

If possible, Sylvia's stomach sank further.

SYLVIA: THANKS, I'LL PASS IT ON TO THE OFFICIALS.

She'd just started striding in the direction of the royale control center, when another message chimed in. With a mental command, she projected the holo message, but it was from Kit's boyfriend, not Ezren.

JABARI: HEY, COACH LONG, ARE THERE TECH ISSUES GOING ON OVER THERE? KIT AND DEAN'S FEED HAS BEEN AT A STANDSTILL FOR SEVENTEEN MINUTES. THEY'VE NEVER STOPPED FOR THAT LONG IN A RACE BEFORE, AND I HAVEN'T SEEN THEM APPEAR ON ANY OF THE OTHER ROYALERS' FEEDS EITHER.

Sylvia's jaw tightened, nausea threatening to upend her.

SYLVIA: STAND BY, I'M FIGURING IT OUT AND I'LL LET YOU KNOW WHEN I HAVE AN UPDATE.

But where was Ezren? She checked Simon and Bex's feed again, trying to reassure herself that the odds of a coordinated attack from Calderon had to be low. It could just be an accident. There was no proof it was planned, violence, or foul play, and it looked like the Amarals weren't far from the recommended path. Unless the relay comm in the cave wasn't working... in which case, they could be anywhere. But although it was a little spotty for the other racers, Kit and Dean seemed to be the only ones affected to this degree.

Sylvia strode straight into the center of the spherical grouping of holos with a swirl of people inside until she was face to face with Crion's Ambassador Purcell.

She gave a perfunctory bow, making sure her goggs were recording in case she needed to reference this conversation later. "I hate to disturb you, Ambassador, but are you aware of the situation with the Amarals?"

The man's mustache twitched as he pulled his attention away from the holo in his goggs. "Yes, don't you worry, Coach Long, we're tracking it closely."

Every muscle in her body tensed as she tried not to think of the two other times she had heard someone say almost those exact words. "Is it a communication issue?"

"We have confirmed that it's not a problem with our equipment, and without a mayday signal it seems unlikely that the royalers' gear would be malfunctioning either." He turned his attention full on her, his wrinkled face soft. "Our best guess is that they're dealing with an injury, waiting for a suit tear to regenerate, or taking rest."

"But they've been silent on comms," Sylvia replied, gesturing to her goggs.

"Which is common for teams in a resting moment," Purcell replied patiently.

"This is a short race, and they just started three hours ago— there's no way." An explosive heat began to gather in Sylvia's skull. "If one of them was hurt, the other would be dragging them across the cave by their ankles."

Purcell held up his doughy hands. "The cold can do strange

things to people, and it's only been twenty minutes since they stopped."

Sylvia ran a hand across her face, trying to keep her building rage in check. "Look, I appreciate the optimism, but can I please get an official to go out and check on them?"

Purcell's puffy mouth tightened briefly before he offered her a placating smile. "We'll note your concern, Coach Long, but as I'm sure you well know, unless they activate their mayday signal, or it's triggered automatically, we can't send someone out until they're officially disqualified or three hours have passed."

Sylvia narrowed her eyes, the heat under her skin nearly unbearable now. While she knew how desperate Crion was to be recognized as an official member of the race royale community, she'd hoped common sense would prevail over the letter of the regulations. "Ambassador Purcell," she began, working to keep her voice even. "If you wait three hours to send a check, and it takes you two hours to reach their location, their dead bodies could've been cold for over *five hours* before you find them."

Purcell straightened as if she'd threatened him. Suns forbid anything happen to throw a wrench into their precious new race royale. "The Amarals are professional race royalers, are they not? With top-of-the-line gear that passed the pre-race check? If there was a problem, their transponders would automatically send a mayday, and I trust you coached them on how to manually send an emergency signal should they encounter strange circumstances."

"Strange circumstances have certainly come up before," she snapped, the fire now billowing out of her. "And the mayday signal did not prevent my royalers from being driven off the course on life support."

His face purpled. "A problem that stemmed from Belethea's own heart."

"Does the source matter?" Sylvia raged back, her hands flying. "When two royalers could be at risk at this very moment?"

Purcell straightened with a deep breath, his muddy brown gaze studying her before flicking to the wide-eyed race organizers around them. "Sylvia," he said, his voice softening as he took her arm and gently tugged her to the side. "There are 120 royalers out there right now who are at risk. We are using all our limited resources to monitor and make sure they are safe—especially as they come up on the wheels, which as you know, is historically the deadliest portion of the race royale. While external foul play is a possibility, it is exceedingly rare. Our staff is closely tracking the situation and has run a risk probability analysis that tells us that the most likely incident is a non-life-threatening injury preventing advancement, or possibly even detainment in an ice pocket. Those are both things that can wait the allocated time until we collect them." His wide mouth pursed, chatter resuming around them as someone enlarged the holo of a three-team scrap. "If we break the regulations, especially for Belethea, it will only heighten scrutiny with calls of cheating, preference, etc. Belethea already escaped one disqualification attempt after last year's debacle; do you really think you could survive another?"

Fod.

Sylvia deflated, her indignant fury seeping out under the weight of his logic. "Thank you for your attention to this matter. Please contact me if the situation changes." With that, she turned on her heel and strode out. Though his lack of concern still incensed her, technically everything he'd said was true. If they interfered, they ran the risk of another intersystem

uproar, and Belethea did not need that again. But where were—
The ding of a goggs message interrupted her thoughts.

Ezren: We're fine, Sylvia. What's going on?

Foster: Does this have to do with the Amarals' feed?

Sylvia let out a relieved sigh, at least one of the knots in her back loosening.

Sylvia: Short answer, yes. But don't worry, I'm taking care of it. You just focus on enjoying your New Year!

Okay, she'd laid it on a little thick, but she didn't need them worrying about this when they were supposed to be taking a few days off from their council duties. Their shoulders were already heavy enough. She could carry this bit. It was her job as coach after all.

But if they were okay, that only gave more credence to Purcell's pitch that it was just a normal hiccup. Still... she couldn't shake the feeling that something was wrong. At a bare minimum, the Amarals should've been squabbling. Casolla knew they'd barely stopped since arriving on Crion.

She pivoted at the door to the viewing room, taking one last look at Grady/Guns as they ran through the dark, still solidly in fourth place. From Micah's VSoc updates in her goggs, they were already heavily favored to podium. And she knew in her bones Kit and Dean should've been up there with them. Their navigation, crisis management, and speed were too high not to be unless something drastic had happened.

And if it had, they needed help.

She shifted her weight from foot to foot, trying to weigh the risks. If she interfered, she could be risking Grady/Guns' disqualification, her coaching position, and intersystem criticism crashing down hard on Belethea itself.

But if she didn't, she could very well be leaving Kit and

Dean to die. Her lips pressed together as she remembered Foster's screams coming over the feed when he discovered Genevieve two years ago—her smashed face before the feed had gone dark.

Yeah. She was not going to let that happen again.

Not to *her* royalers.

And if Calderon was back to his sadistic games, they had to know—with Foster and Ezren sitting next to him in the council, it would only be a matter of time before he came after all of them.

The decision cooled to steel in her chest, and she sprinted down the hall. If she was going to run headfirst into a royale without anyone knowing, she needed a doubles partner.

T-plus 2.25 hours after race start

SHIRO

SHIRO STOOD in the tiny room, silently congratulating himself as Turnip rubbed against his leg, preening after she'd successfully upturned the champagne bottle from the bedside table. In an enormous stroke of luck, it hadn't shattered, and he managed to nestle it firmly between the pillows.

While the venue had indeed been full yesterday, most of the politicians' schedules were too busy to stay more than one night—especially after they realized Sterling/Hart weren't actually here. And after tracking down five different venue officials, he'd finally found one he'd been able to talk into letting him check in with zero notice.

That said, the tiny one-person bed with the closet-sized bathroom wasn't exactly the opulent suite he had in mind. He'd definitely have to find another way to deliver on that bath he'd promised Sylvia. But one wall still sported a fantastic view of the mountain range, it was only a few rooms down from her royalers, and most importantly, they'd be alone.

And surely he could make some adjustments to freshen it

up. With a mental command, he connected his chip to the walls, flicking through the holo options as he tried to decide which one said "please let me spend the rest of my life with you." He knew there were a few large greenhouses on site and wondered if they might have anything as extravagant as a rose. It was rare and would be fritzing expensive, but it would be worth it to see the look on her face.

Now the real question was, how did he propose? He settled on a mountain holo that would give the impression that the room was open to the outside world, the aurora splayed across the ceiling. Should he propose in here where it was private? Or take her out to one of the mountain tops for the view? Turnip mewed at his ankle, and he crouched to scratch her behind the ears. Maybe he could put the ring around Turnip's neck some-how? After all, Turnip was *theirs*. The beginning of their little family. The pink cat raised her chin as he scratched her neck in just the right spot.

Knowing Turnip though, the cat would run off with the ring just to be cheeky.

Turnip looked up at him with huge eyes, and his lips twisted. "Do you think she'll say yes?"

The cat chirped in what sounded suspiciously like a, "No."

Shiro grimaced. "That seems to be the consensus." And a part of him knew it could happen. Maybe Sylvia really was married to the royale. Maybe she wasn't ready to make such a lasting choice. Or maybe she simply didn't believe in such an old-fashioned vow.

He straightened, looking out at the mountains again. Thinking of falling asleep and waking up next to Sylvia every day—on Crion, Belethea, Otho, in space between here or there. He took a deep breath, steadying himself at the heady possi-bility of being with her always—a dream that had been tanta-lizing him for months, and one he could no longer postpone. In the end, it didn't matter if his odds were slim, he had to ask her. He wanted it with every fiber of his being, and he had to know if she felt the same way.

And maybe, if he timed it just right—if he asked in just the right way, the 'verse would align, and she'd say—

A chime in Shiro's goggs interrupted him.

SYLVIA: WHERE ARE YOU?

He couldn't suppress a smug smile.

SHIRO: CHECKING INTO MINOR MIRACLE ROOM SIXTEEN.

SYLVIA: I'M ON MY WAY TO YOU. WE HAVE A PROBLEM.

Shaft. Shiro had the royale update ticker playing along the bottom of his goggs, but he hadn't seen anything emergent pop up. He brought up the standings:

Grady/Gunderson: 4th

Amaral/Amaral: 58th

Shiro winced, rubbing a hand across his stubbled jaw. Well, that wasn't good, but there weren't any reports of a mayday. Were the Amarals lost... or was there something else holding them back? *Someone* else?

Shiro's mood blackened with a curling unease as he shifted back to the messages the CIF had sent him on their mystery stranger from the day before. He hadn't come up in their database, and they had yet to dig up anything on him. Which almost certainly meant he was a syndicate man. Shiro's pulse kicked in his chest even as he tried to reason with himself. Just because he was bad news didn't mean he was here for them.

But... he didn't really believe this ice-rock was big enough for two unrelated mysteries, and if anyone knew how to find trouble on the most remote planet in the system, it was the Belethean Race Royale team.

With a resigned sigh, he took one last look at his hard-won room, and stepped into the hall. The door had barely slid shut behind him when Sylvia careened into the hallway. Alarm spiked through him at her wide eyes, and his body went tense. Something really was wrong. Her mass of curls jostled around her cheeks as she flew into his arms, her voice hushed.

"I think Kit and Dean are in trouble." Her hands gripped his elbows as the words tumbled out in a rapid whisper. "They haven't moved in a half hour, their feed isn't updating, and the race officials won't do anything about it since there are no other signs of distress. I need to go get them without anyone finding out."

Shiro let out a slow breath, his mind whirling. "That long?"

Though he was still relatively new to the royale business, he knew there were few possibilities that could explain something like that, and none of them were good. They had to get to them fast, that was obvious, but getting to them without anyone knowing... Coming back to the moment, he realized he hadn't answered her yet. Her brown eyes searched his, shining with both fear and that fierce determination he knew all too well.

"Okay." He tucked one of her curls behind her ear. *Beautiful.*

"Shiro, will you help me?" Her voice was barely audible over her shaky breaths, and the apprehension in her tone unbalanced him. Sylvia was rarely uncertain—and he never wanted her to be unsure about him.

"Of course. You don't even have to ask." He folded his arms around her waist, taking in the cams he'd already noted in the hallway as the bones of a plan formed. It was probably a bad idea, but it was all he had on short notice. He pressed his lips to the shell of her ear, his voice barely audible. "Have you told anyone else?" Sylvia shook her head as he dragged his cheek along hers until their lips brushed. "Good."

Sylvia drew back, her rainbow brows knitting. "Shiro, I'm serious."

"I know." The corner of his mouth lifted, and he smoothed the wrinkle between her brows with his thumb. "But do you trust me?"

She held his gaze for a beat, and the tension in her jaw eased before she gave him the smallest of nods.

"Then I need you to follow my lead." With that, he swept her into his arms, deepening the kiss. Whatever reservation Sylvia had before melted as her body molded to his, her hands tunneling through his hair. Their mouths ignited as he pushed her against the wall, a low noise vibrating through her lips. Chaff. He wished they had more time. Wished he could fall into this. But... their royalers had to come first.

He bent and lifted her into the air, her legs wrapping around him in a way that lit his body on fire. Okay, maybe this hadn't been the best idea. Suns, she was about to unravel him right here in the hallway. With what had to be celestial strength, he pulled away from her mouth, her eyes dark and her breath ragged. They were totally going to continue this later.

"You have at least one royale pair doing well, and there's nothing you can do for them now anyway," he managed, his voice rough. "What you really need is some time to relax."

Shiro: Wink. Wink.

"What'd you have in mind?" She cocked an eyebrow at him, and chaff, this woman certainly knew how to play along. If she was unsure of his plan, she gave no indication.

Opening the door to their private room with a mental command, he carried her inside, letting the door hiss shut behind him. The lights came slowly to life, and he gave her one last soft kiss. "Okay, I'm going to stop, but for the record, I want to remember exactly where we left off so we can pick back up later." He let her slip through his hands to the floor, not missing how her gaze lingered on his lips just a beat longer.

Recovering herself, she adjusted the purple goggs in her

curls, disguising her smile with a smirk. "Okay, I think I might agree if you tell me what that was all about."

He moved to his military duffel of supplies he always carried with him—where Turnip currently nestled on the canvas. He picked up the small pink cat and handed her to Sylvia before digging through the bag. "*That* was so later, if someone asks where we were, we have plausible deniability." He handed her a small pistol, absurdly glad she'd made time to let him train her with it over the past few months. He threw their topsuits out after it, his own revolver already holstered beneath his jacket.

"Okay, but where do we go from here?" Sylvia put Turnip down on the bed before methodically stripping out of her top and skirt. It was a sight Shiro sorely wished he had more time to absorb as he threw off his own clothes. Instead, he shoved his legs into the topsuit, the nanomaterial weaving around his body as he slid a knife into his boot.

"Out the window of course." He glanced in her direction, making sure she was looking away as he slipped the ring from the box into the inside pocket of his topsuit. Common sense said he should've left it, but in the last few days, he couldn't bear letting it out of sight.

"But we're three stories up." Sylvia looked hesitantly down as she slid her arms into her long, tight-fitting sleeves, the tactical topsuit he'd gotten her taking on a neutral gray. "And there will be cams out there too."

"There will, but not as many, and I've already mapped out their blind spots." It had been a pleasant distraction from the Amarals' bickering on the three-day journey from Belethea, even if the security around here was sorely lacking. Now, he was at least a little glad of it. "The trick is to be seen and unseen exactly when we want to be."

Sylvia slid her gun into the holster at her thigh. "Are we going to fly out?"

"No, there's no way they wouldn't notice us taking off. We're going to drive."

"And how are we going to get a vehicle?" Sylvia asked, pulling her helmet over her curls as he strode to the window, a smaller pack of supplies strapped to his back.

He popped open the glass with a practiced hand, the cold wind seeping into the room. "They've modded some land-sea vehicles for research purposes, and as luck would have it, they're parked right around back." He anchored the retractable rappelling rope to the glass and attached it to his suit.

"And how do you know that?" she asked, peeking nervously at the ground.

Shiro stepped to the edge of the floor-to-ceiling window and pulled her to his chest. Snaking an arm around her waist, her hands curled around him in a way he'd never get enough of. "Because you hired me to know. Now, don't scream." With that, he leapt out of the window.

CHAPTER 6

T-plus 2.5 hours after race start

SHIRO

SHIRO HELD Sylvia close as they plummeted in the Earth-like gravity. In another breathless second, the rope slowed their fall until Shiro's feet ever so softly touched the ground. He yanked the rope and it detached from the anchor, falling straight into his outstretched hand.

Sylvia lightly slapped his chest. "A little more warning next time?"

He couldn't help but grin. "Oh, don't tell me that Sylvia Long, the Belethea Race Royale coach, is afraid of heights?" He pulled her along with him as he skirted the cams on the way to the land-sea trucks, trusting the softly falling snow would eventually obscure their footprints. With a thought from his chip, he connected to the cams on their path and implanted his looping protocol just in case.

"It's less the heights and more of the falling unexpectedly off of them." Her gaze skewed to the line of vehicles in the open hangar, uncertainty creasing her brow once more. "How are we just going to drive away with one of these? Won't someone know it's missing?"

"They might know it's missing, but they won't necessarily know it was us who took it." Shiro scanned for a guard, but of course everyone was in the warm building watching the royale. He gestured to the research vehicles with a proud wave. They weren't as large or as sturdy as the Tac-Vs he was used to, or even a storm truck, but they sported retractable skis as well as wheels. It would do. "Feel free to choose your steed, madam."

Her eyes narrowed behind her goggs. "You'd better be taking this seriously."

He tensed, thinking of the ring stashed in an inner pocket of his suit. "Of course I am." And he was, but if he explained how grave he actually believed the situation to be—Sylvia would panic. And he couldn't have that. Not when he expected the royalers weren't the only ones prowling Crion's caves today. He needed her sharp.

"Fine. I'm driving." Sylvia strode up to the nearest truck and flung the door open.

"I wouldn't have presumed otherwise." Shiro grinned as he let himself into the passenger side. "I have to admit I'm looking forward to seeing you in your royaler element."

Sylvia connected her chip to the holodash. "I'm guessing you have the starting code."

Shiro linked his chip to the vehicle and inputted his CIF agent override. "You could say that."

Sylvia groaned as the truck came to life around them, a course lighting up the holodash. "Suns, are we really stealing a truck right now in the middle of a royale?"

"If this is the most of our worries, I think we'll be doing well," Shiro said, settling into the protective netting. Sylvia shot him a glare, and he reached out and squeezed her shoulder.

"Seriously, you can relax. As a CIF agent, I'm authorized to requisition civilian vehicles for official purposes."

A flash of pleased heat glinted in her eyes. "And *this* is why I hired you." With that, she engaged the skis and the vehicle slipped out of the small research town—in the opposite direction of the royale. "I'm going around the mountain range. Hopefully it'll keep us above suspicion if someone did see us, and it should only cost a few minutes." They'd scarcely made it out of the outskirts before she slammed on the accelerator and the vehicle took off in a spray of snow.

Shiro sank back into the netting with the bark of a laugh. "Are you sure you didn't just want an excuse to take a joyride?"

"I wish." Her eyes crinkled, sparking with light as the research vehicle tore across the ice, navigating around rocky outcroppings and drifts of snow.

"This is how you got into royaling, right?" Shiro asked.

Sylvia nodded. "On calm days, my family and I would take out our jetbikes and just go driving along the surface." He could hear the smile lilting her voice. "I fell in love with it. The control right under your fingers as the world rushes by around you—like you're flying. Like you could leave everything behind."

He rested his hand on her leg, drinking her in. Her stiff posture thawed under his touch, but her eyes remained focused as she adjusted the grav controls. His other hand drifted to the ring sitting just above his heart. "I don't think I've seen you go out for a joyride since I've known you."

She snorted. "It doesn't exactly fit in the schedule."

"But it should," he pressed, skimming through the holodash control panel. "You should be able to make time for this. For the things you love. For you."

She shook her head, but her eyes had softened. "With what time, Shiro?"

"With the only time we have." Finding the setting he was looking for, the vehicle's roof turned transparent, letting the green and purple lights from above spill down on them.

Sylvia's voice dropped, the aurora shimmering in her eyes. "But what if I step back, and they fail?"

Her leg trembled beneath his hand, and Shiro wished he could fold her in his arms. "Whether you step forward or back, they will eventually fail, Vi. But you know better than anyone that progress isn't straight. Sometimes you have to take two steps back and scope out the big picture before you go forward —especially when we all know how far you can go."

For a moment, they were silent, the snow pelting the windshield with soft slaps as Sylvia skirted the edge of the mountain range—pointed in the right direction, but the Amarals were still almost two hours away.

"I was just supposed to be the social manager, you know," Sylvia said, her voice barely audible over the rev of the engine. "It was supposed to be a job I could handle until I finished my business degree and figured out what else I wanted in my life."

"Life surprised you, and you surprised it right back." Shiro smiled. "It was pretty much the same for me. The CIF offered to pay for my school in exchange for service. It was my ticket out of the Dreitis tenements, but I never really thought I would be CIF forever."

Sylvia's glance flicked toward him. "What did you want to do after the CIF?"

"I don't think I ever thought that far ahead. Maybe that was part of the problem." He laughed. "I just figured I'd know it when I saw it." His gaze shifted back to her, the ring pressing into his chest.

She met his eyes with an inscrutable blend of emotions. "So you're telling me you didn't always dream of doing security for a few Belethean royalers?"

"I didn't think I'd ever be that lucky." He winked at her, and she let out a soft scoff. He sobered, looking ahead again. "Besides, I think we're continuously deciding what to do with our lives. It's not something that happened one day and then we're done. We're always changing."

"And that's the issue!" Sylvia gestured with a hand at Crion, as if its snowy surface was the root of the problem. "How am I supposed to plan with so much change?"

"Sometimes you can't." Shiro squeezed her leg. "You just have to adapt to what's coming at you."

"Sounds like you've been thinking a lot about change lately," Sylvia said, something in her tone guarded.

He looked at her again, and their gazes locked, heat zinging between them. "I have." Shiro opened his mouth to say more, but realized if he continued down this path, he was going to ask her to marry him right there in the vehicle. And what if she said no? That would certainly make their rescue mission awkward. Instead, he patted her thigh, and leaned farther back in the netting. "Like I said, it's normal."

He had to focus on this first. Then the rest of their lives could come later, even if he desperately wanted it to start right now.

For the next two hours, he gave her constant updates on the race royalers as they got to their vehicles. He relayed the make and model of the jetboat that Grady/Guns had chosen as well as who was ahead of and behind them. But Kit and Dean did not move, and the VSoc theories were growing increasingly vocal.

In light of Martina Navarro's outburst the day before, most thought the Amarals themselves were staging some kind of protest against Calderon. A few others said they were never-terras sabotaging Belethea from the inside. And then of course, there were the claims that they were dead... but Shiro tried to downplay those.

Still, the tension in Sylvia's shoulders grew with every moment the Amarals didn't move, and when they finally made it to the mouth of the cave, Shiro, personally, never wanted to get on VSoc ever again. How did Sylvia deal with that every day?

Sylvia brought the research truck to a skidding halt at the narrow mouth of the cave—only big enough for two or three people to enter shoulder-to-shoulder. "We have to run from here, but they're only about thirty minutes from this entrance."

Their last known location. It was another thought Shiro didn't say aloud. "Right." Shiro grabbed his bag and stepped out into the snow, immediately sinking up to his knees. The cold seeped into his skin as the nanitelattice of his topsuit whirred into action to keep him warm. "Make sure your gun is charged and ready." Okay, that wasn't encouraging either, but there were some things he really couldn't skip over.

Sylvia checked her gun, and he nodded approvingly as she took the safety off. She obviously didn't need him to tell her what the stakes were out here, and technically their bolt-ammo could only incapacitate. But he'd bet their ride home that whoever was inside the cave would not be returning the favor.

"And you make sure you keep an eye on your topsuit." Sylvia gave him a stern look through her goggs as they jogged toward the cave mouth. "Your strain tolerance hasn't been the same since Otho. And I really don't want a repeat of your nearly dead body being dragged to the paramedic chair." She shuddered.

Shiro's lips twisted—his memories of that moment blurry from his near miss with death. By the time Simon and Bex had gotten him back onto the ship, between his injuries and the toll of his topsuit, his heartbeat had failed as they boarded, and

Simon had to resuscitate him. Luckily, Sylvia's screams had shocked him to the edge of consciousness so that he'd been able to pass on an electric jumpstart. It was an experience he didn't want to repeat either.

"This place is way more tame than Otho. The air is actually breathable here, so the only thing our topsuits are regulating is a temperature differential." A *sizable* temperature differential, but nothing like Otho or even Belethea. He nearly slipped as he stepped onto the slick floor of the ice cave, the lights of their suits illuminating the deep blue walls.

"Okay, but you're also twenty-nine now."

"Oh, don't rub it in. You're only two years younger."

"Exactly." Sylvia curved to the right, her goggs projecting their route on the ice in front of her. "Neither of us are of royaling age anymore."

"Which is too bad." Shiro kept his voice light, even as his eyes swept the darkness, his fingers brushing his gun. "I think we would've made a great team."

Sylvia turned another winding corner that opened into a wide cavern. "Team Tanaka/Long? It's not exactly catchy." Sylvia slowed as they approached a deep hole in the ice. "This is where they were last seen."

Shiro's gaze swept the cavern again, but he could detect no trace of anyone. "Be careful." He turned on both the thermal and audio sensors in his goggs.

"I need to check if they're down there." She leaned over the hole in a way that made his stomach flip, and he gripped her arm to steady her.

"No." She straightened with a frown. "My sensors reach straight down to the bottom. No trace of heat."

Shiro opened his mouth to say something else when the faintest echo registered in his goggs. He pulled Sylvia to the edge of the wall, tugging her into a crouch behind an ice shelf.

Her wide eyes met his, and he tapped a finger against his helmet for silence before pointing to his ear.

Sylvia moved to peer over the top when he pulled her down again.

SHIRO: TRY NOT TO MOVE. MY GOGGS WILL RECORD THEIR TRANSCRIPT FOR US. HERE.

He connected his chip to hers, hoping that whoever it was wouldn't have the presence of mind to be tracking emissions.

UNIDENTIFIED VOICE 1: DID YOU FIND THEM?

UNIDENTIFIED VOICE 2: NAH, THEY'D ALREADY MADE THE VEHICLES.

UNIDENTIFIED VOICE 1: BUT WE WERE WAITING FOR YOU FOR SHAFTING HOURS! WE WERE SUPPOSED TO GET ALL FOUR OF THE DUSTMITES.

UNIDENTIFIED VOICE 2: WELL, I DON'T KNOW IF YOU NOTICED, BUT THEY'RE FODDING FAST.

UNIDENTIFIED VOICE 3: EH, WHO CARES. THIS SHOULD BE ENOUGH TO GET THE MESSAGE ACROSS TO THOSE STERLING/HART CHAFFERS.

Shiro and Sylvia shared identical wide-eyed stares. *Fod.* Whatever this was, it certainly wasn't an accident.

UNIDENTIFIED VOICE 2: AFTER THE SHAFT THEY PULLED ON OTHO, THEY SHOULD BE GETTING WORSE.

UNIDENTIFIED VOICE 1: THEY WILL. JUST LET THE BOSS WORK AND MAKE SURE WE MAKE IT LOOK NICE.

Shiro squeezed his eyes shut for a brief moment. Definitely a syndicate. *Suns, please don't let one of those kids be dead.* Sylvia gripped his hand, and he opened his eyes, pressing her hand between his own and looking straight at her.

SHIRO: NO MATTER WHAT HAPPENS, DON'T PANIC. OKAY, VI? YOU CANNOT PANIC.

Sylvia nodded, but he could see her chest pumping wildly as the glow of suit lights played over the ice.

UNIDENTIFIED VOICE 1: AND MAKE SURE IT'S SOME-WHERE SOMEONE WILL FIND IT TOO. LAST TIME WE DID THIS THEY DIDN'T FIND 'EM FOR MONTHS.

UNIDENTIFIED VOICE 2: WELL WHOSE FAULT WAS THAT?

Shaft. They were coming closer, and there were at least three of them. But who were they? Was there a possibility it could be a group of rogue royalers?

His lips tight, he slipped a stealth hovercam from his bag and slid it across the ice. Keeping the hover thrust minimal to mute the sound waves, he mentally maneuvered it along the ice in the direction of the voices. They only had minutes before they or the cam were discovered, but they were the crucial seconds he needed to evaluate the threat in order to accurately react to what came next. And they could be the seconds in which their survival was decided. Either way, if they didn't get more information, they were totally chaffed.

Sylvia's eyes remained locked on him, her grip like steel on his arm as he ever so slowly edged the cam into the long flat section of the chamber. His heart hammered in his chest as the feed swiveled to take in the three men in nondescript black topsuits on the ice. Not posing as royalers then. That spoke to a brazen lack of fear that was *not* in their favor.

But worse was the fourth person lying on the ice. The person that was registering zero heat on the cam's thermal sensor.

Because they were dead.

CHAPTER 7

T-plus 5.5 hours after race start

SYLVIA

SYLVIA BIT down hard on a scream, her limbs bucking in a visceral reaction to the body on the ice filling her goggs. Shiro's arms locked around her, preventing her from flailing.

SHIRO: SHH, IT'S OKAY. IT'S NOT ONE OF OURS. IT'S NOT A ROYALER. SHHHH.

Sylvia sucked in huge, strangled breaths as she tried to focus on the image to confirm. Shiro had let the cam hover high enough to get a better view of the body. And sure enough, the man's face was clear as day. So clear, in fact, that she recognized him. Because it was the same man who had tried to kill them four months ago.

Ambassador Oliver York.

His body was blue and stiff with the cold, his unnaturally young face frozen in time forever, and his limbs stiff in a tattered spacer jumpsuit. No injuries marred his body that she could see, but his expression was stuck in one of horror—his jaw open impossibly wide and his eyes so huge they looked too large for his face.

Whatever had killed him, she had a feeling it had been long and painful. But even worse than that were the blood streaks beside him.

Sylvia: Whose blood is that?

Shiro's expression was tight behind his goggs, any signs of his usual levity gone.

Shiro: I don't know. Can you read what it says?

Sylvia: IT SAYS SOMETHING?

But no sooner had Sylvia thought the words than she realized that they had indeed managed to arrange the blood into letters.

Welcome to Casolla's stage, Sterling/Hart. Sometimes people just disappear, so consider this my gift to you. I look forward to working together.

—Crow

Sylvia's jaw dropped, confusion scrambling her thoughts. So that's why no one had seen York in months? He was *dead*?

Sylvia: It's a message. Is Crow a part of the Kalashnik? I thought they were working *with* York.

Beside her, Shiro had gone deathly still, his face white behind his goggs.

Shiro: Unfortunately, the Kalashnik are hardly the biggest or worst syndicate out there. Which is why they were lackeys for someone like York. Sometimes politicians and people of power recruit the smaller syndicates to do their dirty work. But with the bigger syndicates, the food chain goes the other way around.

A chill ran up Sylvia's spine that had nothing to do with the cold.

Sylvia: Who's Crow, Shiro?

Shiro's gaze met hers with an apology between his long lashes.

SHIRO: THEY CALL HIM THE KING OF CASOLLA, SYLVIA... HE'S AS BAD AS IT GETS.

Sylvia slumped against the ice shelf.

SYLVIA: AND HE WANTS FOSTER AND EZREN TO WORK FOR HIM.

Her gaze flicked back to the feed as the men began to move out of the frame, and Shiro nodded.

SHIRO: THE QUESTION IS, WHERE ARE THE AMARALS?

Sylvia sucked in deep, silent breaths the way Shiro had taught her. She'd promised him she wouldn't panic, but this was so much worse than she'd first imagined. Calderon was a known quantity—awful, yes—but at least they knew what they were dealing with. At least he operated under the semblance of reason. But the Crow...? Sylvia watched in horror as the men cut away York's suit, leaving him bare on the ice and his body... oh suns.

SHIRO: DON'T LOOK AT IT, SYLVIA.

But Sylvia couldn't tear her gaze away from the thousands of grotesque cuts riddling his skin, a sob edging her breath now. Yes, he had died a slow and painful death. And those men were going to find them any second. She was no champion royaler, no CIF agent—she couldn't do this.

SHIRO: SYLVIA!

Shiro took her helmet in his hands, his dark eyes boring into hers.

SHIRO: LOOK AT ME, I'M GOING TO GET YOU OUT OF HERE. YOU TRUST ME, RIGHT?

Sylvia took in another breath, forcing herself to calm as she stared into the dark swirl of his eyes, fierce and hard.

SYLVIA: I TRUST YOU COMPLETELY.

SHIRO: GOOD. NOW, I NEED YOU TO KNOW, IN YOUR BONES, THAT YOU'RE GOING TO MAKE IT OUT OF HERE.

Sylvia did not miss the "you" where there should've been a

"we," and she'd be chaffed if she let these thugs not only take her royalers but Shiro as well. Her brows knitted, and she drew herself up straight, placing her hands over his. She was scared, yes. But she'd been scared many times before, and chaff, when she was used to multi-tasking twelve royalers' schedules at once, she could handle this one thing.

SYLVIA: I THINK YOU MEAN THAT WE'RE GOING TO GET OUT OF HERE.

Shiro's eyes crinkled.

SHIRO: THAT'S MY GIRL.

UNIDENTIFIED VOICE #1: GET THE OTHER TWO AND BRING THEM OVER HERE.

Sylvia shifted, her gaze returning to the men now retreating into a darker part of the cave.

SYLVIA: SO WHAT ARE WE GOING TO DO? THEY MUST HAVE KIT AND DEAN, RIGHT?

Assuming they were still alive. She couldn't even voice the thought.

SHIRO: I DON'T KNOW. THIS IS AN UNPREDICTABLE SITUATION WITH AN ORGANIZATION WE KNOW IS CAPABLE OF BOTH TORTURE AND DEATH. WE HAVE TO GET THEM OUT.

SYLVIA: THEY'RE COMING THIS WAY.

Shiro swiveled the cam to follow them, and in the glow of their suit lights, Sylvia could just make out two prone forms. *No.* She buried her face in Shiro's shoulder, her chest squeezing the breath from her lungs. She was the one who'd taken them out here. Hot tears gathered in her eyes behind her goggs. If only she had—

SHIRO: IT'S OKAY, LOOK, SYLVIA, THEY'RE ALIVE.

Struggling for breath, Sylvia glanced back to the feed where the cam reported normal vitals on the two limp bodies dragging across the icy cave floor. *Thank the suns.*

UNIDENTIFIED VOICE #1: HEY, WHOSE CAM IS THIS?

SHIRO: SHAFT.

Shiro drew his gun, and Sylvia pressed herself lower against the shelf.

UNIDENTIFIED VOICE #3: IT'S NOT OURS, BUT IT'S SHORT RANGE.

UNIDENTIFIED VOICE #2: TRACK THE SOURCE.

Their words turned Sylvia cold. What should they do? Should they run? But then what did that mean for Kit and Dean? Shiro turned to her, resting his free hand on her knee.

SHIRO: WE HAVE ABOUT FORTY SECONDS BEFORE THEY FIND US.

Sylvia tried to put something coherent together but came up with nothing, her hands shaking as she slid her gun from her thigh holster. While she knew how to use it, she'd never had to —and she was finding that to be a huge discrepancy now.

UNIDENTIFIED VOICE #1: IT'S COMING FROM INSIDE THE CAVE. SPREAD OUT. THEY'RE NOT FAR.

UNIDENTIFIED VOICE #2: THE OTHERS ARE ON THEIR WAY—WE DON'T KNOW HOW MANY WE'RE DEALING WITH.

Sylvia's head jerked toward them, her whole body shaking now. They were trapped in this cave, and in forty seconds they'd be dead. Shiro's hand guided her chin until their gazes met again.

SHIRO: SYLVIA, I NEED YOU. ARE YOU WITH ME?

Sylvia let the gravity of his eyes pull her in, the steadiness of his hand ground her. Her fingers tightened around her pistol, and she gave a firm nod.

SYLVIA: I'M WITH YOU.

SHIRO: I'M GOING TO KNOCK OUT THEIR LIGHTS AND MOVE IN TO DRAW THEIR FIRE. TURN ON YOUR THERM AND TAKE THEM OUT AS THEY REVEAL THEIR POSITION. YOU CAN DO THIS.

Sylvia shifted her grip on her weapon, turning the thermoscan on her goggs. He was depending on her shot. If she missed, he was as good as dead. His trust in her weighed on her shoulders, grounding her to the icy floor—she could be strong for him. She *had* to be.

Two more figures strode into the cave, and as one, the men fell silent.

Shiro: The pulse will knock out their chip transponder for about twenty seconds and force them to communicate verbally.

Sylvia: But there's five of them now.

His eyes crinkled as he slipped a small metal device from his bag.

Shiro: And the odds don't get any better, darling.

Sylvia: Why are your plans always so bad?

He attached the metal disk to the grip of his gun and squeezed her knee.

Shiro: I love you.

Sylvia: You'd better come back.

His gaze shifted to the darkness as his free hand rubbed a spot on his chest.

Shiro: Just don't shoot me, please.

With that, Shiro leapt out from behind their shelf, dashing across the cave as someone gave a sharp bark of warning. The device on Shiro's gun triggered with a deafening click, and the men's lights winked out. Her ears already ringing, Sylvia forced herself over the side of the shelf, keeping her aim steady.

The heat signature of the men's bodies lit up in her goggs as well as the Amarals' limp forms. Though she knew York's body lay next to them, he didn't appear on her display. Because he was dead. The word echoed through her. *Dead. Dead. Dead.*

The men dove for cover, yelling to one another as they tried to pinpoint Shiro's location, and the crack of gunfire blasted through the cave. *Shaft.* That better not have been him.

The ring of the shot centered her, and she homed her crosshairs on a man who stood still a beat too long. She pulled the trigger back smooth, and the shot impacted the man straight in the chest, bringing him to the ground. A shout spurred another flurry of movement, and Sylvia moved to her next target, all the men twisting this way and that.

Her shot missed, just barely glancing off a helmet, and Sylvia swallowed a curse.

Gunfire filled the cave now, bright red figures shooting and running in the chaos of the darkness. The din seemed to fade as she focused on her shot, knowing it was only a matter of time before the hitmen found Shiro. Only seconds before the killers' goggs came back on, and they shot both of them.

Breathe. Aim. Fire. Miss.

Breathe. Aim. Fire. Hit. Three to go.

Breathe. Aim. Fire. Miss.

Breathe. Aim. Fire. Miss.

One was shouting and pointing in her direction now. Fod.

Aim. Fire. Miss.

They were coming toward her, bullets spraying across the cave. She flinched as the shots came all too close.

Fire. Miss.

Fire. Miss. Shaft. Two were closing in.

Breathe. Aim. Fire. Hit.

Another shot hit the shelf of ice, and she lurched back in the spray of ice chips. Shaft. Had they hit her? No, no, she was fine. She was—

A body lurched over the shelf, firing wildly down at her. With a scream, Sylvia returned the shot, and the man fell directly on her chest, knocking the gun from her grip. She struggled under his limp weight, her breath rattling in her ears.

There was one more. She still had to get the last one. A light flickered on over the shelf, and she crawled out from under the man. Where was Shiro?

She fumbled for her pistol in the dark when a figure leapt out of the shadows, and Sylvia screamed, raising her hands to defend herself.

"It's me!" Shiro yelled, and Sylvia sagged against the wall. "Are you okay?" Then his hands were on her, patting her down as if he needed physical proof that she was in one piece.

"I'm fine. He just hit the ice." She squeezed him back, her body tingling with adrenaline. "But what about the last guy?"

"I got him, but I have a feeling there are only more on the way." Shiro bent and picked up her gun, handing it to her. "Those were some good shots." Pride shone from beneath his goggs, and Sylvia felt her face heat, even as her body began to shake once again.

"What about my royalers?"

Shiro tugged her by the hand towards where Kit and Dean lay to one side of York's frozen body. "They're all right—just mildly sedated." Kneeling, Shiro pulled what looked like a hand-length cylinder from his pack. "Nothing some stims can't fix."

He jabbed Dean in the thigh with the nano stimulants first before tossing it back in his bag and grabbing another one, stabbing it into Kit's leg.

"How long does it take?" Sylvia asked, her eyes glued to York's stripped body and the bloody message scrawled on the ice. Nausea rolling through her, she took a few shots with her goggs to serve as evidence later.

Shiro didn't get a chance to say anything before Dean let out a long groan. "Why is it so cold? Did I fall asleep in an ice bath?"

Sylvia knelt by his side and pulled him to a sitting position.

Somewhere in the cave, a deep rumble shook the floor. "Dean, we've got to go."

Dean's unfocused gaze swept the walls of ice around them. "No, we're in a royale. We have to finish the race."

"The race is over," Sylvia said, another vibration shaking the ground beneath her feet. What *was* that? "I need you to get up." She yanked him to his feet, only for the giant to sway and stumble as she tried to support his weight. "Shaft. What's wrong with him?"

"It's the sedation," Shiro explained as he gently shook Kit. "Give it a minute."

Kit lurched to a seated position with a gasp. "We have to run. We're behind!" She scrambled to her feet only to nearly fall over before Shiro caught her. "Where's Dean?"

"I'm here, I'm ready," he said, tearing away from Sylvia.

"Hey." Shiro gripped Kit's arm as he reached for Dean. "Listen, it's not safe, we have to get you out of here."

"It's fine," Kit said, yanking her elbow from Shiro. "We've got this."

"No," Sylvia snapped, blocking her path. While she was relieved they were okay, they still didn't have time for their stupid arguing. "You were knocked out, and there are no vehicles left. You missed the cutoff." Kit and Dean stared blankly at each other, her words slow to sink in. "And now, people are trying to kill us, so you're going to listen and do exactly as we say."

For a moment, neither sibling spoke, until finally Dean adjusted his goggs around his helmet. "How did we miss the cutoff?"

Kit's eyes finally fell to York's body only a few paces to their left. "Who the chaff is that?"

"We can talk about it on the way," Shiro said, waving them in the direction of the exit.

"Basically, you were sabotaged." Sylvia pushed them forward as she began to jog. The vibrations were coming consistently now, deepening the foreboding in her gut. "And we need to get out of here before we join Ambassador York in the next life."

"Shouldn't we do something with the body?" Dean asked, glancing over his shoulder.

"I have holos, and I'm already forwarding them out to the people that can spread the word," Sylvia said.

They were full-on running now, and Sylvia's chest sang with the lightness that they had made it. That they were going to be okay.

Then another shot rang out.

CHAPTER 8

T-plus 6 hours after race start

SHIRO

SHIRO FLINCHED as the first shot caught Dean in the shoulder, and he cried out, stumbling before Kit caught his elbow.

"Move!" Shiro shouted, turning sharply to return fire as Sylvia and the Amarals wound around the corner. There were at least three shooters behind them, the curving walls and slippery ice working to their defensive advantage. He squeezed off three quick shots in their general direction, forcing them to dive for cover as he ran after the others.

"We're still ten minutes out from the truck," Sylvia explained as they all bent over to run through a particularly narrow tunnel. "Are we going to make it?"

Shiro glanced at the blood trail Dean was leaving behind— thankfully it wasn't thick enough to bleed out, especially with the nanitelattice of his topsuit already knitting over the wound and providing a natural pressure. Though Dean's face was screwed up behind his goggs and his feet were stumbling, Kit was pulling him along at an insane clip. Even injured, the two were ridiculously fast.

He glanced back the way they came only to find the three men were no longer in pursuit. Which honestly was even more concerning than when they were. "How many exits are there to these caves?"

Sylvia snorted as she got down on her hands and knees to crawl through the narrowest section of the tunnel. "Like a million, Shiro. It's huge."

"Well the good news is, I think we're going to make it out," he said, accepting her proffered hand to let her pull him through the tight squeeze.

She tugged him to his feet, and they ran after the Amarals who were pulling so far ahead, they were almost out of sight. "What's the bad news?"

"The bad news is..." Shiro glanced over his shoulder, his chest heaving with the toll of his topsuit. Suns, his nanite endurance was totally shot these days. "They're not chasing us."

"Well, this is the fastest way to the truck. I don't think they have time to loop ahead."

"But we don't know how many there are."

Kit and Dean were out of sight now, and Shiro swore under his breath.

SHIRO: WATCH FOR AN AMBUSH AT THE CAVE EXIT.

SYLVIA: HOW MANY PEOPLE COULD THESE GUYS HAVE?

KIT: I SEE THE WAY OUT. NO ONE'S HERE. HURRY UP!

"Suns," Shiro wheezed, daylight trickling in from an opening ahead. "What have you been feeding them? I think you picked the right team for this, Coach."

"Well, we wouldn't be Belethea if we didn't have one royale that was totally chaffed up." Sylvia kept pace beside him, a hard glint to her eyes. "It's starting to look like our royalers can't compete without a near-death experience."

Shiro didn't miss the guilt coating her words. "That's not your fault though."

"The Belethea team's safety is my responsibility."

"And you've kept them alive against all odds." He sucked in another ragged breath. "Congratulations."

That finally got a snort out of her. "We really need to get you out of that topsuit."

"Is that your way of telling me I'm getting too old for this?" They'd reached the mouth of the cave, and he strafed the shadows for movement. Nothing. And yet something was vibrating beneath their feet.

"Maybe."

"I think I can be talked into retirement. Settling down with a girl and a cat." He side-eyed her as they stepped out of the cave into the thigh-deep snow but couldn't gauge any change in her reaction. In fairness, he had said some variation of those words dozens of times in the past months.

"Well I—" Sylvia stopped short, the aurora shimmering through the cerulean sky. "What's that sound?" A bone-thrumming vibration sang through the air, and twenty paces ahead, Kit and Dean were already in the research truck. Kit beckoned them with a wildly waving arm as she brought the vehicle to life, the truck already lurching forward on its skis in the deep snow.

Time slowed as Shiro took it in—the modded lunar hopper with the pulse gun streaking from around the mountain behind them—its aim pointed at the giant sheet of white coating the slope above. Its first shot exploding high near the peak, and snow breaking away to plummet toward them. They had seconds... and they didn't at the same time. The ship pivoted toward the research truck as the avalanche hurtled toward them at uncomprehending speed.

SHIRO: DRIVE, KIT!

Kit accelerated before he even sent the message, her survival instincts kicking in as the truck jolted away. The ship's second shot scorched through the snow where the truck had been only a half second before.

DEAN: WHAT ABOUT YOU?

SYLVIA: WE'LL BE FINE—GO!

Shiro aimed at the hopper, firing off a couple shots at the ship with almost no effect. He needed to change his ammunition. Needed—

"C'mon!" Sylvia yanked him toward the cave's mouth, fear and determination melding into a steel façade beneath her goggs.

Shiro focused on her hand squeezing his arm, forcing his legs to move as they lurched through the snow. The mountain's furious rumble rushed down toward them in a blinding white tumult, and the mouth of the cave yawned ahead, but they needed to go faster, faster, faster.

He grabbed Sylvia and leaped forward, skidding across the ice to the cave floor, curling his body around her just as the crush of white enveloped them. Pain crunched through his chest as the force of it propelled him into the wall, blinded by the ivory expanse. The cold weight of it sent his suit into hysterics, his vision going black before another jolt of pain sizzled through him with his suit's resuscitation protocol. He was trapped in a prison of white, snow pressing him against the wall from every angle. But Sylvia. He couldn't feel her anymore.

SHIRO: SYLVIA, WHERE ARE YOU?

SHIRO: SYLVIA, ARE YOU OKAY?

Nothing. He'd lost her. He tried to move but couldn't overcome the overwhelming weight of the snow. How long did they have before they asphyxiated? Then again, did it really matter when there was no hope of rescue? His mind spun and nausea roiled his stomach with what he knew had to be a concussion. Suns, this was bad. Involuntarily, his mind went to the ring tucked away in the inside pocket of his topsuit. He really should've asked her. Why had he waited? Maybe he could still—

His body tensed as he strained to move, but between the unyielding wall behind him and the crushing weight of the snow, all he achieved was another sharp pain in his chest. He didn't even know which way was up. His vision was fading again along with his sense of time, the topsuit's toll reaching untenable levels. With nothing else to do, he let himself give in to it, his mind going blank as time slipped away. Wouldn't it be ironic if the thing that was supposed to keep him alive ended up killing—

His thought was interrupted by a spot of black in the blinding white lit by his goggles. A shuffling and a muffled voice. Wow, these syndicate guys were really intent on finishing the job. Gloved hands reached toward him, seizing his arms and pulling. He gritted his teeth against the wrench of his injuries, trying to prepare himself for whatever came next— trying to summon his strength through the pain.

Only to emerge from the snowbank and fall directly on top of a beautiful woman.

Tears streamed from Sylvia's soft brown eyes behind her goggs as she wrapped her arms around him. "Shiro, thank the suns you're okay!"

He let his head sink against her chest, the relief overcoming him. "Sylvia. Chaff. I tried sending you a message." He managed to roll away, his vision taking in the mass of white where the entrance had been and the tunnel Sylvia had dug out to extract him.

"Our goggs comms are down with the cave entrances blocked." Sylvia rose to a sitting position. "My best guess is that this entire side of the mountain is buried so we need to make it to the north slope to get out."

For a second, he just looked at the icy ceiling, trying to get his concussed brain to take this in. "And the syndicate men might still be in here."

"Unless they think we're dead," Sylvia countered, offering him a hand.

He let her heave him to his feet with a loud groan, pain pulsing through every cell of his body. "Right, how far is it to the other side?"

Sylvia winced as her goggs glowed, a holo of his injuries flicking out—two cracked ribs and a severe concussion. "Not far, maybe fifteen miles." She moved to his bag, got out a painkiller, and jabbed it into his neck.

"Ow." The royaler idea of what "not far" was never ceased to amaze him.

"We can make it in a couple hours." She crawled back through her makeshift tunnel and extracted his gun, pushing it into his hand. "C'mon, let's move."

He didn't resist as she practically pushed him through the tunnel, something frantic about her movements even as her tone remained calm. The knowledge of what they weren't saying pulled taut between them. The chances of his injured body enduring two more hours in the topsuit was slim.

"Do you think the Amarals will make it?" Sylvia asked, her voice quiet as they ran through the winding darkness.

Shiro thought of the modded hopper shooting at the research truck—the ice falling around them. "You have to trust your royalers. If anyone can make it, they can." Sylvia slipped on a patch of ice, and he caught her elbow, only to slip himself. "You picked them because they're the best, right?"

"But they're rookies."

"But you believe in them."

It wasn't a question, and Sylvia fell silent for a second as they practically skated through the tunnels. "I believed in Genevieve Navarro, but I still had to tell her family she died." Her voice was so soft he almost missed it. "I was the one who had to tell Martina." She slowed to a stop before a low tunnel, desperation dark and hard in the depths of her eyes. "I don't want to have to tell the Kit and Dean's parents they're dead too."

Shiro stopped beside her, gathering her into his arms. "Listen, they're going to be okay." He tried for a smile, his ribs aching. "And besides, who says we're going to survive this to tell anyone anything?"

Sylvia snorted, and Shiro's chest lightened as the two of them stooped through the low tunnel. "We'll be fine." Only the slightest tremor belied Sylvia's words. "I have a map. It's not updating, but I can use it to get us out."

"Which is all blime unless the syndicates are waiting for us on the other side instead of a rescue mission." Not to mention the whole topsuits tearing their bodies apart thing. The memory of the pain screaming through his body in the paramedic chair after Otho bolted through him, and his muscles tightened as he straightened to run after Sylvia again. He couldn't stress her more. She would need the confidence if they were to have any chance at all. And even if he didn't make it out, that didn't mean she wouldn't.

But with two hours left to go, he had to find some way to take his mind off the dull pain throbbing through his every pore. Distract them both from thinking too far ahead to the barrel of the gun that might be waiting for them, or the bodies of the Amarals lying somewhere in the scarlet snow. No, they couldn't think about that.

So, he did what he did best. He talked.

"Does this bring back fuzzy memories of your royaler days?"

"You know I wasn't very good."

"You look like you're doing pretty well to me."

"I only competed my final year, and even then, I think we were in the bottom ten teams at the qualifier."

"Sounds like it was a character-building experience."

"Even though we were bad, we always had fun. We were glad just to be on the team—competing. We felt invincible." Her face practically glowed with the memories. "And we always threw the best parties."

"And now you're so strict with your royalers about parties!" Shiro said between ragged breaths. "The injustice!"

"That's because my royalers are competitive! The Amarals were the top recruits coming out of Belethea. A few years ago, they would've gone to one of the spacer teams for sure. We have to provide the right environment for them to succeed. Even though Sterling/Hart won last year, we're still trying to get rid of the loser-image from my time."

"And what are all your royaler teammates doing now?" His head jerked up with a sudden realization. "And who was your doubles partner? Should I be jealous?"

Sylvia laughed, leaning on the ice wall for support. "Back then, we switched up doubles much more often, so we all doubled together at one time or another." Her tone softened with a wistful edge. "But I'm not really sure what they're doing now. Most of them just used the team as a steppingstone to better things before they scattered across Casolla. I've lost touch with nearly all of them." Her breath puffed out with her words as they climbed a steep slope. "Odd how you can be so close with someone, then circumstance can turn you into strangers without a thought."

"Not all the time," Shiro said, distinctly disliking the turn of the conversation.

Sylvia glanced at him with curiosity. "So were circumstances different with your CIF friends?"

Shiro's lips pursed inside his helmet. As a scholarship brat from the Dreitis slums, he'd worked his ass off to earn his peers' approval. But he'd done it, coming out with distinguished marks and laboriously climbing the rungs to classified missions. But then as soon as his honor was thrown in question over the Otho scandal, they'd abandoned him.

They'd all come back of course once he'd cleared his name, and they gave him a few apologetic medals for marring his record with inactive duty. But he didn't have time for fickle friends. Before that, he'd lost his childhood kin to the harsh reality of life on the ass-bottom end of society. Some dead, some with empty lives, others eaten away with bitterness.

Which was all to say, that when he'd met the Belethean royalers, anyone he'd called a friend had become a stranger as well.

But this was supposed to be a light, distracting conversation, so he bumped her with his shoulder. "Eh, that's too far back to remember. I am exactly in the circumstance I want to be in."

Sylvia shook her head with a chuckle. "You don't have to do that, you know."

"Do what? Charm and delight?"

"Deflect." Her gaze leveled him as they jogged side by side. "You can tell me what you're really thinking. We can be serious."

"I don't want to weigh you down. I mean, we *are* running

for our lives, and you're already carrying the figurative baggage of twelve royalers now."

"Maybe I am, and maybe it's hard, and maybe sometimes it makes me want to tear my hair out, but I chose this." Sylvia shrugged. "You know, I've never been the strongest or the fastest royaler, but I always knew I could work the hardest. I knew I could learn to give us the advantage in other ways— chaff, I'm still learning. But one way or another, I can take the weight off. For you and for them. And as much as I love the team, they don't come before you." She glanced at him. "So when I ask how your friends are, you can be honest."

They don't come before you. The words thrummed in Shiro's chest, and he blew out a long breath, feeling strangely light despite the circumstances. "I don't think I've been the best at making the right friends."

Sylvia nodded, the purple light of her goggs glowing off the icy walls. "Until now."

He feigned shock, one hand flying to his chest. "Is this how you tell me we're just friends?"

"Shiro!" Sylvia snort-laughed, his name a giggling groan. "That counts as another deflection."

"Oh, all right." He focused on her to avoid his fixation on the ever-growing pain. "Yes. Somehow, I finally got lucky."

Her eyes met his with a spark, and together they fell into a companionable silence as they ran through the miles one at a time—the minutes crawling by as the pain ratcheted even higher. He snuck another painkiller while Sylvia squeezed through a tunnel again, but it was only dulling the real problem. It would just be a matter of time before he could physically go no farther. But they were so close. So very close.

"We're almost there!" Sylvia said, her voice bright with hope. "We're at the last half mile before the exit, then we can get a message out for someone to come get us. We might even be close enough to the vehicle station to find some shelter."

Shiro nodded, his thoughts fading in and out with the blackness edging his vision. He tried to focus on Sylvia running against the background of glacier blue, but his stare skipped across the violet light of her goggs playing across the curves and spikes of the cave.

Sylvia glanced around the wide cavern as well before turning onto another narrow passage. "This place would be beautiful if we weren't trying to escape."

"That's every royale." Shiro's body had begun to shake uncontrollably, his suit unable to compensate for the cold any longer and sweat soaking every inch of his skin. Still, he made sure to run carefully behind Sylvia to avoid her notice. After all, there was nothing she could do about it. They could only keep moving forward.

"Well, no offense to Crion, but its ice maze is a bit hard to navigate."

"And your planet has death storms," Shiro said, trying to force his voice to be even between his heaving breaths.

"So you prefer the freezing cold?" Sylvia asked, climbing up over an ice shelf to the tunnel on the other side.

His vision swam as he dragged himself after her, his words beginning to slur. "I prefer anywhere you are."

Sylvia laughed. "Oh, c'mon, Shiro, be serious."

"I am." There was no more time. He put a hand on the ring resting against his chest, reaching out to grab her arm. Delirious images skated across his eyes, his mind once again on her. He had to tell her something. Had to.

She turned, her eyes widening as they landed on him. "Shiro!"

"Sylvia, I—" But his next words were lost as he collapsed onto the ice.

CHAPTER 9

T-plus 8 hours after race start

SYLVIA

"MOTHER SUNS!" Sylvia's hands shot out, just barely catching Shiro before he crashed backward onto the ice. "Shiro!" His face had blanched behind his goggs, his eyes closed. She knew without asking it was the strain of the suit failing, but she also knew the only cure for that was to take the suit off—which, down here, would kill him in a matter of minutes. "Shiro!" When he didn't respond, she flipped him over to get into his pack, pulling out a stimulant injector and sticking it into his neck.

He came to with a gasp that sent a flood of relief through her. "Why didn't you tell me it was this bad?" she asked, mentally berating herself for not paying closer attention to him. But she had just figured if he was talking, he must be okay. Apparently one of Shiro's superpowers would be talking until he was on the verge of death.

He let out a low groan as she pulled him to his feet.

"I didn't want to worry you," he said, tension tightening each and every word.

"Didn't we just have a talk about how I can handle it?" She heaved him toward the exit, her body starting to ache from the pain of her own suit. "Is there anything else that you didn't want to burden with me that I should know?" She kept her eyes on the ground, mentally calculating how long it would take her to drag him half a mile at a walking pace. Ten minutes? Eight? Could she be fast enough?

"Um..."

"Suns, there is, isn't there?" Now it was her turn to groan.

"Did I already say that the Crow was going to coerce Sterling/Hart for his own game?"

"Yes, you did say that." Which was actually worse, since that obviously meant he was starting to lose his grip on coherency. "Do you think that's why Calderon wanted them to join the council? As part of this sick little game?"

"They're all playing that game, and if Sterling/Hart don't learn to be the king and queen—they'll be pawns instead."

Sylvia nearly scoffed at the thought of how Ezren and Foster would take that news. Though they'd risen from BRR champions to intersystem ambassadors to BRR council members, they'd taken every step as reluctantly as if it might cost them their lives. And maybe that was closer to the truth than anyone liked.

Sylvia's brow furrowed as she continued her climb, lengthening her stride as they passed another corridor in the warren of ice. But wasn't she guilty of the same thing? Hadn't Ambassador Villegas practically offered her the general manager title on a platter? A position that would give her more power and sway to protect her team, to get them the resources they needed, the VSoc players, and the coaches.

Chaff, she even knew exactly what she would do and who she would ask—as if the decision had been percolating in her mind for months, just waiting for her to be brave enough to take the leap.

Even if the leap took her out of Carmella. Took her away from the team she'd nurtured and been a part of for the last six years. It was time for her "after." For herself, and for her team, she could no longer afford to bend to the inertia of her comfort zone. If her royalers were in danger of becoming pawns, she had no choice but to become a queen as well.

Her decision made, she sucked in a deep breath. "None of those are good sides to be on. Because of course everything in this mess has to be so chaffing complicated."

"Some things are easy," Shiro said, his teeth chattering.

Sylvia let out a chuckle. And this was exactly why she loved Shiro. Because here he was, on the very verge of death, defying everything that had brought them here. The rock to her chaos storm, and she would be fodding shafted if he died on her. She would not let him. "Well, if we were all as certain as you, maybe the 'verse would be a better place."

"Absolutely..." He pulled away from her, wrapping his arms around himself as he leaned against the wall. "But I think I need... just a second for my... body to catch up."

Oh no. Oh no no no. Sylvia wrapped her arms around him, trying to give him some of her heat, but knowing it wouldn't transfer through the suits. "No, Shiro, we can't stop, the exit is right around the corner." She hoped. Suns, she hoped.

"It'll be okay, Vi." He reached out and squeezed her hand with his shaking one.

"I—"

A deep echo through the cave interrupted him, and the hope Sylvia had been holding on to so tightly cracked. With silent footsteps, she peered around the corner just far enough to get a glimpse of four shadows in the mouth of the small opening they'd been looking for.

She ducked back into the corridor. *Shaft.* They had to move.

"Vi, there's something I need to tell you," Shiro wheezed.

Suns, he was out of it. "Shh." Sylvia looked over her shoulder, simultaneously looking for another exit in the map in her goggs. There it was—not far. "Not a good time."

Behind them, the voices grew louder, and she inwardly swore, her mind spiraling as she grappled for her gun. At this point, the hitmen would probably rejoice in killing them—what a great message to strike fear in Ezren and Foster. There were too many to take by herself, but there were so many tunnels, they had at least a few minutes, and there should be an exit right in front...

Sylvia looked up at a huge wall of white.

No. She checked and rechecked her goggs.

"There should be an exit here." Sylvia's stomach dropped, the horrible reality of just how trapped they were dawning on her.

"It's the avalanche." Shiro stumbled forward, some clarity returning to his feverish eyes as he reached out and punched a hand into the snow. He pulled his fist away, but there was only more white beyond.

The floor vibrated beneath them, and a crack spread across the wall.

"They're bringing the whole mountain down." Sylvia tried to swallow, but her mouth had gone bone dry—her throat raw with the freezing air. "That was why the men didn't follow us. They didn't need to."

Shiro nodded. "So they can make it look like a cave-in. Covering up their mistakes."

Which included the Amarals too.

"No," she whispered, staring at the small dent his hand had

made. She looked up to where the sunlight glowed farther up. "I refuse to be some pawn they can sweep off the board."

Stepping into the snowbank, she used the side of the cave to claw herself up the wall, cutting at the snow with desperate waves of her arms as the crack in the ice spread like a ravenous spiderweb. She dug as the pain throbbed through her body, as her fingers went numb and her knuckles stung—until finally, a pocket of light shone through the darkness.

"I've got it!" Widening the hole, she peeked out to search for the syndicate thugs. But their current perch was higher up on the mountain and at least partially sheltered by a chunk of ice. Thank the suns—they needed the break.

Hopping back down, her bubble of elation popped as she saw Shiro lying on the floor. She skidded to his side. "Shiro!"

His eyes opened, a smile edging his voice. "Shh, I thought you said we were supposed to be quiet."

"Chaff." Sylvia resisted the urge to punch his smug face, even as she lowered her voice to a whisper-shout. "I thought you were dead!" She took his hand and pulled him to his feet.

"I told you I just needed to rest."

And in truth, he did look at least a little stronger. She flinched as another thunderous crack shook the ice. "As soon as we get back to that nice private room you miracle-d for us, you can rest all you want." She boosted him through the hole she'd created before clambering out after him. The sky shimmered with emerald and lilac, and Shiro was already peeking over the boulder. He slid back down, his back against the icy rock as he faced her. "Any chance we could find a different exit?"

The ground vibrated beneath them as the cave shuddered with an audible crash. Sylvia stumbled backward in the abrupt landslide, and Shiro grabbed her, tugging her to him and covering her with his body.

He rested his helmet against hers, the tunnel she'd created once again filled with ice. "I'll take that as a no."

Sylvia summoned the last of her energy to peek over the boulder. At least a dozen men fanned out in front of the small shelter of the vehicle checkpoint. Their modified lunar hopper sat next to them, with its pulse cannon firing another shot at the base of the mountain, shaking the ground beneath them once more.

And this time it was Sylvia's turn to fall to the ground, the last shreds of her energy gone, and the pain rushing in as Shiro curled his arms around her. She looked at him, and his eyes crinkled in an apologetic smile. They both knew if she sent an SOS message, the hitmen would be able to pinpoint their location immediately.

By some miracle they had made it out.

And yet it was going to make no difference at all.

CHAPTER 10

T-minus 8.5 hours after race start

SHIRO

SHIRO SAT GATHERING the scraps of his strength as he cradled Sylvia in his arms. Maybe for the last time. The hitmen were certainly looking for them, and it was only a matter of minutes before they picked up on their thermal signatures. The thirteen men were already widening their search pattern, and there was nowhere for him and Sylvia to go but down the mountain.

Which left them only one option: they were going to have to steal a Crow ship.

He chuckled inwardly at the prospect. If he'd been at his best, it would've served as an interesting challenge. Now though, it was bordering on madness. Still, he was in the right frame of mind for madness, and well, bad ideas were his specialty. From his thermal scanners, only one person was on the ship, but if Shiro got control of that gun, he could use it to wipe out the others. High risk, high reward... but mostly high risk.

Which meant he would be the one taking it.

He looked down at Sylvia, her own strength sapped out of her from the topsuit. "They're going to find us," he murmured.

She nodded, but her eyes were strangely blank. Almost dull. Tearing down the ice wall had really taken it out of her. She had at least tried to pace herself, but it seemed she'd given it her all in what she thought was their final hour of need.

"I have a plan, but the odds aren't great," he said.

Sylvia nodded again, her gaze not leaving his.

"I'm going to try to sneak past them and steal the ship." He slid her gun from her thigh holster and folded her hands around it. "Shoot anyone that comes near you."

Sylvia's rainbow brows furrowed, her expression tight behind her goggs. "This is a stupid plan."

"I know." He smiled, his hand rubbing along her back. "But it's the best I've got."

The tension in her expression only deepened. "I thought you said you had something to tell me?"

He thought of the ring again. Of how this might be his last time to ask her. But as much as he wanted to, he couldn't do that when he needed her to focus. "It can wait." He rose to his feet, shifting the gun in his hands as he mentally charted a concealed path through the ice.

"Shiro, don't do this," Sylvia pleaded, slumped against the boulder. "Maybe we can just wait them out. Maybe someone will come for us."

He shook his head, surveying the skies just in case. "We can't bet on a maybe. And if I don't split their fire, it'll be a blink before they find us here."

"But you're hurt," Sylvia said, her voice painfully small. "You barely made it out of the cave."

"That really makes no difference when we only have one option." He smiled beneath his helmet. "I have enough in me left for this." He turned to her, unable to still the tremble of his body. Suns, he was going to be a terrible shot. He took one last painkiller out of his bag and injected it into his leg. It was bordering on an overdose, but that was the least of his worries right now. "Before I go, I need you to know that I love you." He swallowed, a heavy sort of nerves stealing over him. He'd faced slim odds before, but not with the love of his life on the line. Not with the future he so desperately wanted resting against his heart and dangling just out of reach at the same time. His voice dropped to a whisper. "Seriously. You know that, right?"

Sylvia's brown eyes welled, but her words were steady. "I've known it for a long time."

He smiled, his chest finally warming. "Good."

"Almost as long as I've loved you."

Will you marry me? Shiro had to bite back the words on the tip of his tongue, tightening his grip on his gun as he looked at her one last time—wishing he could kiss her. "That's an argument I'd love to have with you when we get out of this."

"You mean *if*," Sylvia said, her helmet clicking softly against the ice as she leaned her head back.

"When," he gently corrected her, his muscles tensing. "I still have something to ask you." And then, he was vaulting over the berm of ice and sliding down the slope.

His topsuit turned a mélange of white and glacial blue as he slid through the snow and ice, aiming for a jagged outcrop. Pausing, he glanced at the nearing men before taking a chance and sliding for the next bit of cover. He was only halfway down before the first shot sent a spray of snow into the air, the crack ringing through the quiet.

Well, so much for sneaking. Still sliding, he returned their fire, praying the aim assist of his tactical topsuit would be enough to compensate for his shaking hands. Four shots and he'd taken one down. He bounced off a boulder and angled in another steeper direction, practically flying down the incline.

Shots peppered the snow way too close, one searing his thigh with heat as it grazed him. But he barely noticed over his thundering pulse, death singing through the air as he returned it in kind—his focus completely on the aimpoint in his goggs.

Shot shot shot. *Another one down.*

Shot shot. *Number three down.*

Shot shot shot shot shot shot. *Four.*

Another bullet glanced off his helmet, throwing him to the side. He just barely managed to pull himself into a shallow crevasse in the ice, his mind spinning as he returned fire, the remaining dozen advancing on him and—

Oh shaft.

The lunar hopper's massive gun was turning in his direction, and he was much—*much*— too far.

He fired a constant barrage, managing to take one more out as his gaze slewed up to Sylvia's hiding place. Maybe they wouldn't look for her. Maybe she managed to get away somehow. His vision spun again as another explosion of white blinded him.

He braced for the massive shot of the lunar hopper, but a man appeared out of the snow instead, kicking his gun away. "It's another one of those Beletheans," the man said into his goggs. "I think he'll do nicely.'"

Were they trying to take him alive? Shiro took a knife from his boot—the last of his defenses—his fingers clumsy as the man smirked at him from under his black goggs.

"Are you the one who botched the job then?" Shiro tsked. "Can I speak to your manager?"

The smirk faded from the man's face, and Shiro lunged for him with the knife, but his body was barely responding anymore. The man knocked away the blade with a cruel laugh and kneed him in the gut. In an explosion of pain from his already cracked ribs, Shiro fell—weaponless and barely holding on to consciousness.

"Yeah, he's done. I don't even know if he's going to make it off the ice."

The lunar hopper rose in the air, and Shiro tried not to think about where he was going to wake up. *If* he was going to wake up. He thought instead of Sylvia. Hers was the face he wanted to see before he died. The person he wanted to think about as he fell into the darkness. He didn't need his life to flash before his eyes. Just her. His love. Their future. A dream, fading fast, but a beautiful one.

The smaller gun on the hopper glowed gold beneath the blue sky, and Shiro's body tensed—ready for the pain.

A bright light flashed through the air, blinding Shiro as something impacted his body. Something blunt and heavy. He opened his eyes to see his attacker had fallen on top of him. Dead. *What?*

The other men turned toward the lunar hopper as it swiveled to take another shot, and then another. Each flash brought a shooter down with a precisely lethal shot. One of the men raised his weapon, aiming at the cockpit, and Shiro scrambled for his gun, pausing for only a second to aim before pulling the trigger. The shot glanced off his helmet, and the man staggered to the side, right before the lunar hopper took him down.

With the twelve men now smoking on the ground, a figure stumbled out of the loading door—her purple goggs bright against her gray topsuit. *Sylvia.* How had she made it down there? He staggered to his feet, meeting her halfway as she tugged him toward the hopper. "I've sent an SOS message, but we need to get you inside before the suit tears you apart."

"I thought I told you to stay put," he wheezed as she pulled him onto the ship.

"Yeah, but you always have bad plans." There was a smile

to her words even as her eyes drew tight with pain. "My plan was better."

And he couldn't even argue as they stumbled into the blissfully warm lunar hopper. "But you could barely move in your suit."

"Neither could you." Closing the boarding door, she tugged his helmet off. "But it turns out, you were right, a little rest goes a long way." With quick hands, she unzipped his topsuit, peeling it down his bare torso. The relief was nearly instantaneous, as if a million burrowing spiders had instantly been ejected from his body. She jogged off, returning a moment later with a warming blanket she found who knew where and throwing it around his shoulders.

Only then did she yank off her own helmet with a relieved groan, sliding her topsuit down to her waist to reveal her sports bra and her brown skin peppered with goosebumps.

He pulled her to his chest, enveloping them both in the warming blanket. "I can't believe you smoked a dozen of the Crow's mercenaries."

She shrugged, her arms wrapping around his waist as she looked up at him, exhaustion lining her face but her smirk still coated with her trademark confidence. "I was trained by the best."

Unable to resist a second longer, he leaned his head down and kissed her. She pressed in closer, and he savored the heat of her body, the fresh rain scent of her hair, and the ecstasy of being so thoroughly and completely alive.

Then the incoming ordnance alarm blared from the console.

CHAPTER 11

T-minus 9 hours after race start

SYLVIA

SYLVIA HAD BARELY REGISTERED the alarm before Shiro lurched to the console. In a breath, he was in the captain's seat, the holo flaring to life in front of him. The lunar hopper pivoted sharply, and Sylvia nearly fell to the floor, the whole vessel shuddering as the cannon discharged.

Leaning against the curved wall, she looked up just in time to see a fiery explosion burst across the green-streaked sky. Beside it, the holodash enlarged another ship streaking down from the atmosphere. Shiro fired the pulse cannon at them again only for the ship to swerve, still hurtling toward them at a mortifying rate.

"Fodding suns, did they bring a whole army?" Sylvia swore, leaping into the other captain's chair. "You focus on defense, I'm driving us out of here."

She slammed on the emergency take-off, the acceleration pushing them back into the seats as the netting snapped out of the chair and encircled them. The ship vibrated as Shiro fired shot after shot at their pursuer.

"Aren't you worried about ammo?" Sylvia asked as they hovered inches over the ground, screaming toward Lumik as fast as she could push the engine. The snow-covered landscape gave way to an iceberg-covered sea, the force of their engine sending ripples through the placid waves below.

"I wish I was worried about that," Shiro said, his focus never wavering from the targeting holo. "But unfortunately, I'm not sure this flight will be long enough to warrant it."

Another explosion rent the air, this one close enough for the blast to shudder the ship. Sylvia swerved from side to side, desperately searching for something that could give them a semblance of shelter. But there was nothing in the flat expanse of sea and snow, and the mountain range was still so far in the distance.

"What can we do?"

"You said you sent out an SOS, right?"

"Is that what drew them to us?" A pang of guilt twisted Sylvia's gut.

"Either that or the bodies of their coworkers." Shiro flashed a smile, the orange glow of another explosion lighting his face. "But hopefully it'll also get us some help."

Sylvia tried to calculate the distance between them and the finish line. Her grip tightened on the manual steering wheel as she swerved hard again, a projectile of some sort splashing into the water. They had to get closer—had to buy more time.

"How long do you think we can—"

She didn't finish before a deafening blast burst through her ears. The squeal of metal sundered the air as the ship foundered, nearly turning over. A freezing wind shot through the cabin, and Sylvia glanced behind her, ears ringing, to find the entire right wing had been torn from the ship along with the wall of the fuselage.

They were going down.

"Topsuit on," she shouted over the racing wind, but Shiro was already tugging his sleeves over his arms. Their helmets were gone though, whipped away with everything else that wasn't tied down. *Shaft.*

Shiro fired another shot from the cannon. "How long do we have before we're grounded?"

Sylvia shook her head, struggling to keep the vehicle aloft. "I don't know. Thirty seconds? Can you bring them down?"

"They're pulling out of range." He fired another shot anyway. "How far are we from Lumik?"

"You don't want to know." Sylvia desperately maneuvered them for the shoreline, but they were way too far out. She would have to land them on one of the icebergs—which really meant crash them on what was essentially a floating ice mountain. Survival odds weren't looking good.

And yet, with the hull already skimming the water, she was out of time.

"Brace for impact."

Shiro sat back, and she killed the engine, dropped the flaps, and engaged the reverse thrusters. The force of their deceleration sent Sylvia forward into the netting, and she gritted her teeth as she tried to manually maintain their balance. Normally, lunar hoppers were easy to maneuver and could land on a postage stamp bay in a crowded hangar.

But with one wing...

They skidded across the ice, and Sylvia dropped the boarding ramp, pointing them straight toward one of the white peaks. They ricocheted off the incline, the boarding ramp now digging into the ground as they just barely stopped not twenty feet from the cliff-like edge.

Sylvia let out a long breath, only to choke on the smoke pouring from the engine.

Shiro's hand gripped her elbow as he hauled her toward the open boarding ramp. "We have to get out of here."

Sylvia wanted to tell him they'd freeze out there without their helmets but couldn't decide if that would be a better or worse fate than suffocating inside. Shiro towed her off the plane, downwind of the burning engine but still close enough to feel its heat.

"Well at least we're closer than we were." Shiro forced a smile as he wrapped his arms around her, shielding her from the wind.

Sylvia's gaze remained on the black dot in the gorgeous Crionian sky. A black dot that was decidedly getting bigger. The hitmen were coming back for them. So much for escape. In reality, they'd just been buying time since that first moment they'd seen the mercenaries in the cave. She could only hope the Amarals had been able to get away. That they'd warn Foster and Ezren.

She looked up at Shiro, who was now staring at that ominous ink blot in the sky too. If it weren't for her, he wouldn't be here at all. Wouldn't have run out in the middle of a race royale on a hunch. Wouldn't be on this icy, beautiful planet. Wouldn't be attached to a Belethean team that had a black mark next to their name. And yet she couldn't bring herself to regret that he was here—with her.

"I'm sorry," she said, her voice thick with desperation.

"I'm not." He smiled down at her, his dark eyes soft as he cupped her face with his hands. "I'm counting it as a joyride."

A pang of regret squeezed Sylvia's heart—how had she not taken Shiro jetbiking across the Belethean surface? How had she not made time for that? For him? For her? Still, with Shiro's thumb stroking her cheek, and the ship roaring above, there was no time for regrets. So, instead, she grinned back at him. "Me too."

Another light flashed in the sky—a shot fired—and Sylvia buried her face in his chest, her tears freezing in her eyelashes. But when the explosion came, it was from far above them. As one, their gazes jolted upward to find a ship had rammed into the oncoming vessel, and both were plummeting in a twisted mess of fire and steel.

Sylvia's mind was still trying to comprehend this impossibility, when it became devastatingly obvious that the wreckage was coming straight toward them.

"*Run!*"

Together they turned, making a break for the far side of the iceberg, but only made ten long strides before the ships collided with their floating island, and the world tilted. The force of impact threw Sylvia forward, her hand sliding from Shiro's as she sailed through the air, and straight into the freezing sea.

The cold enveloped her in an icy fist, punching the air from her lungs as she kicked to the surface—her suit going into overdrive to compensate, but doing nothing for the heat lost in droves from her head. She surfaced with a gasp. *Shiro!* Where was Shiro? Not in the water. That was good, wasn't it? Suns, she hoped he wasn't in the water. She clawed the waves for something—*anything* to get her away from the cold threatening to immobilize her. Her body started to shake with violent tremors as she cut at the water toward the ice floe.

She had to keep moving forward. If she stopped, she would die. But just as her fingertips brushed the ice, her body seemed to give out, every muscle seizing with the pain of her suit's overdraw. She let out a shrill scream, knowing even after she'd escaped death so many times—this end was sure to be as painful as the others.

Black edged her vision as a splash drew her gaze—more debris? Ice?

"Fod, it's cold." Shiro's voice cut through her daze just as two strong arms encircled her and pushed her onto the shelf of ice.

Sylvia wished she could've said the relief was immediate, but in reality, there was nearly none. "Shiro! Why are you in the water?"

He hauled himself onto the ice next to her, his body now shuddering just as violently as hers. "To get you."

"But..." She didn't even know what to say to that. Instead of just her, they were *both* now soaked and shivering on a sliver of ice. In the end, all she could do was scoot closer to him. "I think I could use one of your bad plans right about now."

"Don't worry." His eyes glinted beneath his frosted lashes. "I have a feeling we won't need one."

She was about to ask him what he meant when another familiar voice cut through the air. "Here they are! I found them!"

Sylvia looked up to see none other than Simon Grady in a jetchute, descending onto their tiny raft of an ice float.

"Well, you guys look a little worse for wear." He took off his helmet and unceremoniously shoved it onto Sylvia's head. "That should help."

"How are you here?" Sylvia asked through chattering teeth as Bex made a running landing right next to them.

"Well, you did send out an SOS call." Bex's voice was as calm as if it was just another Tuesday.

"But you were racing." Sylvia's gaze raked the sky for more danger.

Simon yanked off Bex's helmet next and shoved it onto Shiro's head. "Well, we grabbed the silver medal first, and then we got the SOS message."

"You came in second?" Now Sylvia was considering the possibility that she might be dead, and this was all just some kind of weird post-death hallucination.

Shiro raised an eyebrow at them. "Tell me that wasn't our lunar hopper you just totaled."

Simon rubbed the back of his head with a chuckle. "Well, I mean, was it really our fault that you didn't get a ride with some guns on it? The ship was the only weapon we had."

"There was no way we would've been able to get close without them shooting at us anyway," Bex added, her own eyes on the sky. "But that should be all of them."

"Which is great and all," Shiro said, sagging to the ground. "But how are we going to get off this ice cube now?"

"C'mon, kin." Simon flashed his trademark smile. "Our coach is Sylvia Long. Our ride should be here any minute."

Sylvia was about to ask what that meant when a land-sea research vehicle careened off the shore into the sea. The same one she and Shiro had requisitioned hours before.

"The Amarals." Sylvia gasped, tears stinging her eyes. "They made it."

"Chaffing royalers." Shiro's laugh bordered on manic. "I'm beginning to think you lot can survive anything."

"They got caught in the avalanche, but the vehicle survived." Bex helped Sylvia up as the research truck pulled alongside their chunk of ice. "So they decided not to move until they heard from you or us."

Simon strode over to open the rear door. "Yeah, they sat in the truck together, not moving for three hours."

"I'm more surprised they survived that than the avalanche." Shiro groaned as Bex hauled him to his feet, guiding him to the back seat.

But as soon as Kit and Dean stepped out of the car, Sylvia wrapped her wobbly arms around them. "I'm so proud of you." She turned to take in Bex and Simon. "All of you." Her brows knitted. "But I can't believe you put yourself in danger for us! I'm supposed to do that for you, not the other way around."

"But... we're still glad you did," Shiro added with a wry glance.

"I think we can all agree it was worth it." Kit smiled.

"Yeah." Dean, one arm in a makeshift sling, helped Sylvia onto the seat next to Shiro. "You said it from the beginning, right, Syl? On this team, we take care of each other."

Kit tucked two warming blankets around Sylvia and Shiro in the back before sliding in next to her brother in the front while Grady/Guns took the middle.

Sylvia and Shiro returned their helmets to their rightful owners before once again peeling off the draining topsuits and replacing them with the warming blankets.

"I don't think I ever want to put one of those back on," Sylvia said, her bottom lip still trembling. "And while I'm making demands, I also never want to be cold again."

"I'll see what we can do." Shiro pulled her closer, both of them in scarcely more than their underwear.

Sylvia marveled in the warm circle of his arms, still disbelieving that they were finally safe. "Did we really make it out, Shiro?" She glanced at the luminescent sky through the translucent roof once more, the royalers' good-natured arguments filling the cabin in the rows in front of them.

He wrapped her hand in his large one. "I think we did. It looks like you still have that superhuman royaler in you. I'd always wondered where it came from. Now I know."

She raised a brow at him. "And it looks like you have it too."

"You must be rubbing off on me."

"That's common between doubles." Sylvia lifted her chin to where Bex, Simon, and the Amarals were bickering about the best route to return to Lumik.

Shiro looked at something in his hand before turning toward her, a strange nervousness fluttering through his eyes. "What if I wanted to be your double for life?"

Sylvia nearly snorted, kicking at their discarded topsuits by their feet. "I thought we'd just decided we never wanted to run anything close to a royale again?"

Shiro swallowed, his gaze earnest and his voice low. "I want to be your double in everything. The one who's always got your back. The one you always come to when you're in trouble. When you need something. When you need anything. Even if it's just a private room or a hot bath."

Sylvia stilled, her eyes flaring wide and her heart squeezing as she realized exactly what he was saying. What, in fact, she now grasped with sudden clarity, he'd been hinting at for the past month. "Shiro..."

"I was waiting for the perfect moment, and I'd heard Crion was beautiful, so I thought it might be the perfect place." He looked around the cabin, the royalers obliviously chattering in the front, and the two of them trembling in their underwear in warming blankets—bruised, battered, exhausted. "But after the last few hours not knowing if I'd get a future with you, I don't want to wait another second to start it. So..." Shiro's dark eyes swirled as he produced a small diamond ring from his hand, and Sylvia's eyes nearly bulged out of her head. "Sylvia Long, will you walk beside me in this crazy life? I can't promise we won't have bad plans or packed schedules, or that Turnip won't knock over the coffee twice a day, but as long as you're with me, it sounds like our kind of perfect." He paused, Adam's apple bobbing. "Sylvia, I love you more than all the stars combined." He sucked in a long breath, his voice whisper-soft with palpable hope. "Will you marry me?"

And Sylvia officially stopped breathing, every thought running through her head fully inadequate for this moment, but not one doubt. "But Shiro..." He froze and Sylvia gave him a shaky smile, glancing around the cab again. The royalers were still completely oblivious, but they were all warm and safe as they hurtled under the green and purple shimmer dancing across the sky. "This *is* the perfect moment." His shoulders sagged with relief, his eyes sparkling with a wide smile. "And I would *love* to marry you."

Then Shiro's lips were on hers, his grin breaking through the kiss as Sylvia laughed through the happy tears streaming down her face.

"Wait." He slipped the ring on her finger, and leaned his forehead against hers. "*Now*, it's perfect." He wiped a tear away from her cheek with his thumb.

But Sylvia couldn't take her eyes off the tiny diamond ring glinting in Crion's starscape of lights. "You were carrying this with you the whole time?"

Shiro smiled, a nervous, relieved laugh bubbling out of him. "When I tell you I couldn't stop thinking about it—I almost asked you in the cave ten times over." He ran a thumb over her finger as if he couldn't believe it himself. "I know it's old-fashioned, but... my grandmother gave it to me."

"It's an old-world ring?" Sylvia gasped. They had fallen out of fashion on spacer ships, where loose articles were a danger and materials were scarce. The only ones that survived had been passed in secret over generations. And apparently this one had come from his late adoptive grandmother—the one who'd saved him from the streets of Dreitis. The enormity of what sat on her finger stole the breath from her lungs. "Shiro, this is too precious—I don't need—"

"I know." He laid a hand over hers. "My grandmother said these days, we don't need a symbol to pledge our souls to the love of our life." He gave a sheepish shrug. "But sometimes it helps. And when *you* are the most precious thing that's ever happened to me, this... is just a ring."

And Sylvia was kissing him all over again, their barely clothed bodies twining together as she drank him in, knowing she would never possibly get enough of him. Even though they were hurting, and there was so much darkness and danger in the world, somehow it had brought her the anchor that kept her sane, the man she trusted before all else, and the one who'd filled her heart with a love she always thought fictional. "I'm yours forever," she whispered.

"And I'm—"

"Hey." Simon leaned over the backseat, eyeing the two of them suspiciously. "You two have been weirdly quiet back there, and I don't think Sylvia's checked her VSoc once. Are you okay?"

Shiro let out a long, full-bellied laugh, and Sylvia hid her own giggle in his neck.

"What's the joke?" Kit asked, peering back at them from the front seat.

"No joke." Sylvia straightened, flashing the ring on her left hand. "We're getting married."

And then the car erupted with four people screaming and cheering and talking at once.

Sylvia laughed along with them, wiping the tears from her eyes as Shiro kissed her brow. And in that moment, after surviving uncountable near-death experiences in the past few hours, with her royalers filling the cab with their joyful shouts, and the love of her life pressed in close beside her, Sylvia was completely lost in the moment.

And she'd never felt more alive.

CHAPTER 12

T-plus 16.75 hours after race start

T-minus 15 minutes to midnight
Shiro

HOW THEY MADE it to the New Year's party, Shiro had no idea. In the span of the last seven hours, he'd been debriefed, an investigative team had been dispatched to the cave to dig out York's body, he and Sylvia had spent three hours each in a paramedic chair to mend their damaged bodies, Sylvia had gotten her hot regenerative bath, they'd filled Ezren and Foster in on what happened, Shiro had gotten the CIF to assign another agent to Carmella until they got back, the Belethean royalers had been part of no fewer than thirty-four interviews both about their finish and the unexpected race interference, and he'd fed Turnip. At which time, she'd managed to spill his recovery drink twice.

Because of course she had.

Now somehow, it was fifteen minutes to midnight, and they were in the ballroom, dressed to the nines—because even if the Crow had ruined their morning, he sure as chaff wasn't going to ruin their New Year.

Shiro looked to where Sylvia stood. *His fiancée.* She stared out the wall of windows to the colors dancing across the sky, a dreamy smile on her face and the ring—his ring—glinting on her hand. *His fiancée.* Gorgeous as ever in her laced corset, short ruffled skirt, and tall boots. *His fiancée.* He'd never get enough of it.

He handed her a bright blue drink with a pink umbrella in it, as was the Belethean royaler tradition. Her team had placed today after all. "There must be a lot going down on VSoc right now. Are you sure you don't need to be giving interviews and managing updates?"

Sylvia's smile glided over to him, strangely serene. "I made some announcements earlier, but Micah and Jabari are on it so I know they'll be able to handle everything between them."

He sipped from his drink and raised an eyebrow. "Any big announcements I should know about?"

"Nothing of the personal kind." She hid a smile behind the rim of her glass. "But I did send a message to a coach I think would be perfect for next year." Her grin widened with unmistakable pride. "I think she's going to accept."

He straightened. "Belethea's getting a new coach?"

"Shh!" Sylvia scooted closer, her eyes wide. "Nothing's official yet."

"What does this mean for you?"

"You mean for *us*?" Sylvia plucked the umbrella from her drink, twirling it between her manicured fingers. "It means that next year, I'll officially take on the general manager title and hire on a few more permanent administrative and security positions and any other help the team needs to grow. Then when Bex, Foster, and Simon all age out of race royales, I'll also officially move out of Carmella for the first time in six years." She chuckled to herself. "It's definitely time." Her grin widened as Turnip mewed by her ankle, and he could've sworn the tiny pink cat was scheming to knock the drink right out of his hand. "I'll have more time for some jetbike joyrides with my fiancé and then..." She turned to face him, running a finger up one of his suspenders. "Maybe we'll move into an apartment across the street?"

And as Shiro looked into her warm brown eyes, he could've sworn he went weak in the knees. Though he'd thought it a hundred times already, it was the first time he'd heard it from her lips.

"Maybe we should get married right now." He made a show of looking around the party. "There's so many people here, surely one of them could give the Casolla blessing."

Sylvia laughed, a beautiful warm sound like a balm to his still sore body. "No, we can't rush. My family would kill me if they weren't at the wedding."

The thought of a wedding sent Shiro's pulse thudding all over again. This was real. Sylvia was real. She would be his, he would be hers, and he didn't think he'd ever wanted anything more. "I can hardly wait."

She turned her back to him, and he put down his drink so he could thread his arms around her, burying his face into her neck. "We're really growing up, aren't we?"

"The ache in my bones from the topsuit overdraw certainly says so," Shiro said with a wry grin.

"Royales were always such a huge joy in my life." Sylvia set her drink on a nearby table, placing her hands over his. "But I never dreamed moving on could feel so right."

Shiro nodded against her hair, breathing her in. "Because we have so many joys ahead of us."

"You know, that sounds like a pretty good plan."

Shiro's chuckle rumbled against her back as he placed a soft kiss on her cheek.

With the party bubbling around them, they sank into

comfortable silence, his gaze sweeping the dance hall once again. All four royalers sat in a tight knot, dancers whirling around the ballroom floor as an orchestra played in the corner, extra security patrolled the door, and no mystery faces popped up in his goggs.

For now, they were safe.

"Sylvia Long!" an imperious, demanding voice called, just as a hovercam flitted in front of them. "This is the Royaler Review. What can you tell us about the blood message left next to York's body? Is it true Ezren and Foster are working with the syndicates now? What does this criminal sabotage mean for the sanctity of the race royale institution?"

Shiro resisted the urge to hurl the hovercam across the room, and Sylvia stepped calmly—*definitely too calmly*—in front of the hStudioSelf. Shiro tensed, bracing for her reaction. With the Royaler Review, there always seemed to be a fifty/fifty chance she would either punch him in the face or reignite their long-standing feud with any manner of snarky remarks.

But tonight, she only lifted her chin. "I'm sure it means nothing good, but if you'd like to hear more, you can schedule an interview with the Belethea team VSoc managers found on our channels."

"What about your royalers? Do you think Grady/Guns might have a chance to win the BRR? After the Amarals incident, what do you have to say about the rumors Belethea might be cursed?"

Shiro's eyes narrowed, his words barely above a growl. "I don't think it's a curse when we know who's responsible."

Sylvia's smile tightened with a nod. "The royale season is young, with plenty of excitement for Grady/Guns and the Amarals still to come, but for now, it's New Year's Eve, and I'm going to dance with my fiancé."

With that, Sylvia led Shiro to the dance floor, leaving the reporter gaping in their wake. With a mew, Turnip tipped over their umbrella drinks right onto the reporter's shoes before prancing off toward the Belethean team.

Sylvia covered a snort with a cough. "I forgive Turnip for all the other drinks she's spilled in the last four months. It was obviously just training for this moment."

"Smart cat," Shiro murmured as he placed a hand on Sylvia's waist, taking her other hand in his. "But I thought you said you weren't giving any personal announcements."

"I suppose I couldn't help myself after all." Sylvia's gaze fluttered to the ground with an abashed smile. "I'm too happy."

And Shiro's chest nearly burst as he spun her in time to the music. "Me too." Off to the side of the dance floor, Simon was crowing about how their next race would be the win, while Kit and Dean argued heatedly that they hadn't gotten a true chance yet. Shiro dipped Sylvia just as a one-minute warning to midnight chimed in their goggs. With a shared grin, he pulled her upright and led her outside onto the heated open deck.

He wrapped an arm around her, tucking her into his chest as they gazed up at the aurora skipping along the mountain peaks. And while it had been an exhausting and unbelievable day, he couldn't help but marvel at it all. Though shadows still waited for them between the stars, there was a breathtaking beauty to the darkness too—an ethereal blaze across the night that would forever burn here.

The thirty-second warning chimed in his goggs, and Sylvia turned toward him. "So I've heard when the bells strike midnight you're supposed to kiss the person you want to keep kissing."

"Is that what you've heard?" Shiro grinned at her. "Well I'll take any and every excuse to kiss my fiancée."

Sylvia gripped his lapels, her expression suddenly earnest. "You know, you really have changed my life. I don't think I would've had the courage to go out there today, to move on, to grow if it wasn't for you." She rested her forehead briefly on his chest as if in prayer. "I'm thankful for you, Shiro Tanaka, and for whatever part of this crazy 'verse brought me to you. I'm thankful for that too."

He sucked in a sharp breath, gathering her in his arms as the clock began to count down in his goggs. "I know a lot of awful things happened this morning, but just know that the moment you said yes made this the happiest day of my life... no matter what comes before or after. You and me together—that's all that counts. Even if we had a million lifetimes, I would marry you in every single one."

Sylvia melted in his arms, her brown eyes soft below her rainbow brows. "I love you, Shiro."

With that, the bells rang in their goggs, and Shiro pressed his lips to hers—her mouth warm and solid and beautifully familiar against his. The only lips he would ever kiss again. And even though he couldn't deny that something churned in the dark—waiting for them in the blackness between the stars— he could savor this perfection. This love. This joy. That belonged to them and them alone.

Turnip mewed from inside the door, pawing at them through the glass, and they pulled away with matching smiles. Then together, they laughed and danced and held each other until long after the bells stopped ringing and the cheers quieted.

Until it was just the two of them swaying along with the lights of a new world dancing across the sky.

ACKNOWLEDGMENTS

Okay, so this book was a wonderful surprise! When I wrote *Into the Fire*, I thought it would be the last in the series, so it was so exciting to get the request from Whimsical for more of Sylvia and Shiro!

So of course, thanks so much to Whimsical Publishing for believing in these characters and this series. Also thanks to our *Into the Fire* street team for getting this series out in the world so we can spend more time in this 'verse! Thanks to my beta readers and critique partners: Mindy, Maddy, Caleb, Erin, and Martha for helping me make this story the best that it can be.

And forever thanks to my wonderful family—to my husband, parents, and wild boys for always cheering me on. I love you all endlessly.

And to everyone who has offered their encouragement over the years—in person, on social media, in your reviews—thank you so much for keeping me going on this writing journey. I so hoped you enjoyed coming along on this adventure with me, and I can't wait to share what's in store for these characters in book three!

ABOUT THE AUTHOR

Hayley Reese Chow is the award-winning author of Odriel's Heirs, Into the Churn, and other upcoming YA adven- tures. When not head over heels in a bookish world, she's also a full-time engineer, USAF reservist, avid traveler, and super nerd. Hayley currently dodges hurricanes in Florida with two small ninjas, her long-su#ering husband, and her miniature rage-hound. To see what she's working on next, check out hayleyreesechow.com or VSoc at @HayleyReeseChow.